Mighty Mighty MONSTERS

THE MISSING MUMMY

STONE ARCH BOOKS

a capstone imprint

Mighty Mighty Monsters are published by
Stone Arch Books, A Capstone Imprint, 1710 Roe
Crest Drive, North Mankato, Minnesota 56003
www.capstonepub.com

Library of Congress Cataloging-in-Publication Data
O'Reilly, Sean, 1974-
The missing mummy / by Sean O'Reilly ; illustrated
by Arcana Studio.
p. cm. - (Mighty Mighty Monsters)
Summary: The monsters take a field trip to the
museum, where they befriend a mummy.
ISBN 978-1-4342-3218-2 (library binding)
ISBN 978-1-4342-4609-7 (paperback)
1. Monsters—Juvenile fiction. 2. School field trips—
Juvenile fiction. 3. Mummies—Juvenile fiction.
4. Graphic novels. [1. Graphic novels. 2. Monsters—
Fiction. 3. School field trips—Fiction. 4. Mummies—
Fiction.] I. Arcana Studio. II. Title.
PZ7.7.O74Mi 2012
741.5'973—dc22
2011003444

Printed in the United States of America
in North Mankato, Minnesota.
062012
006827R

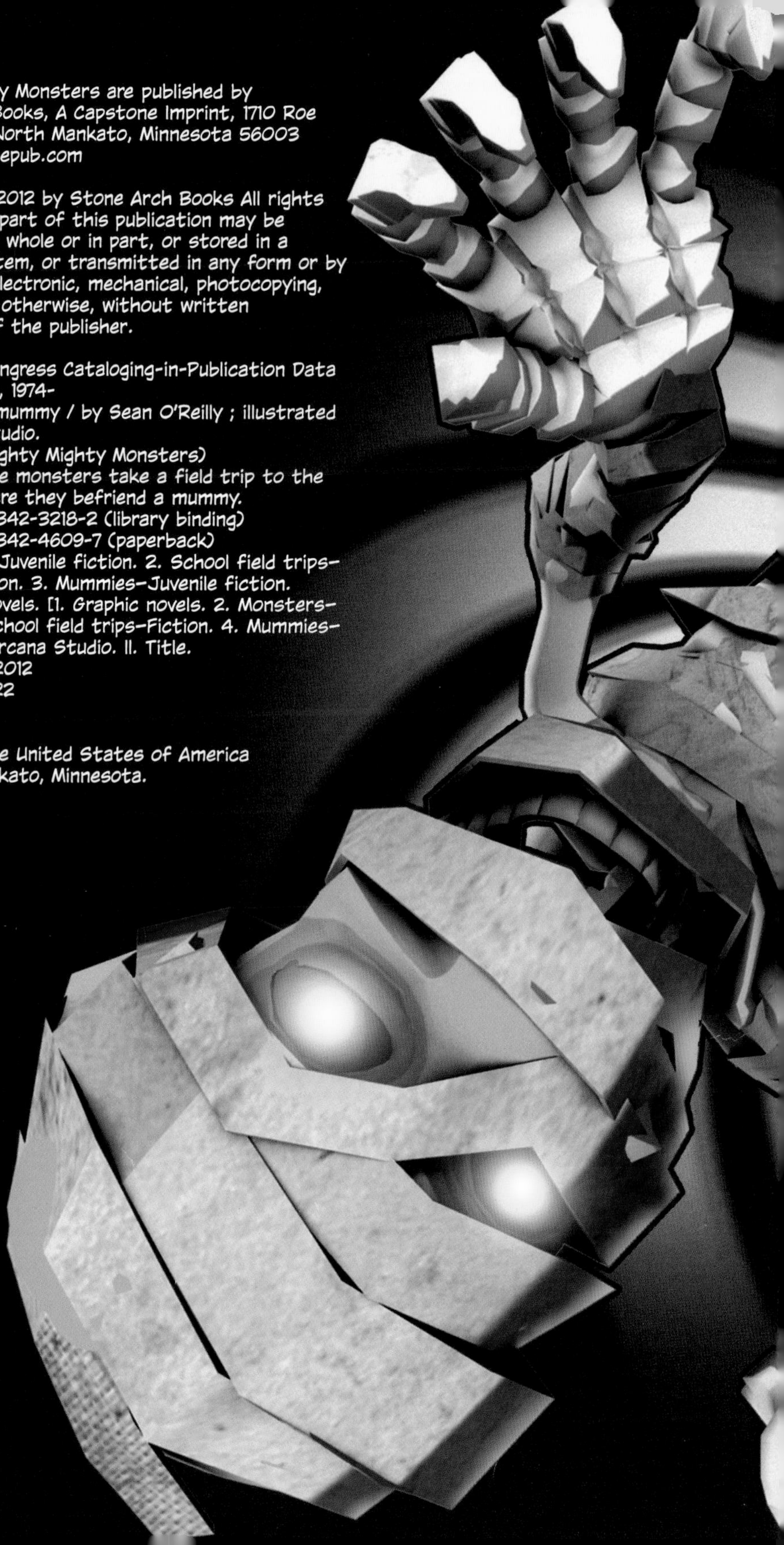

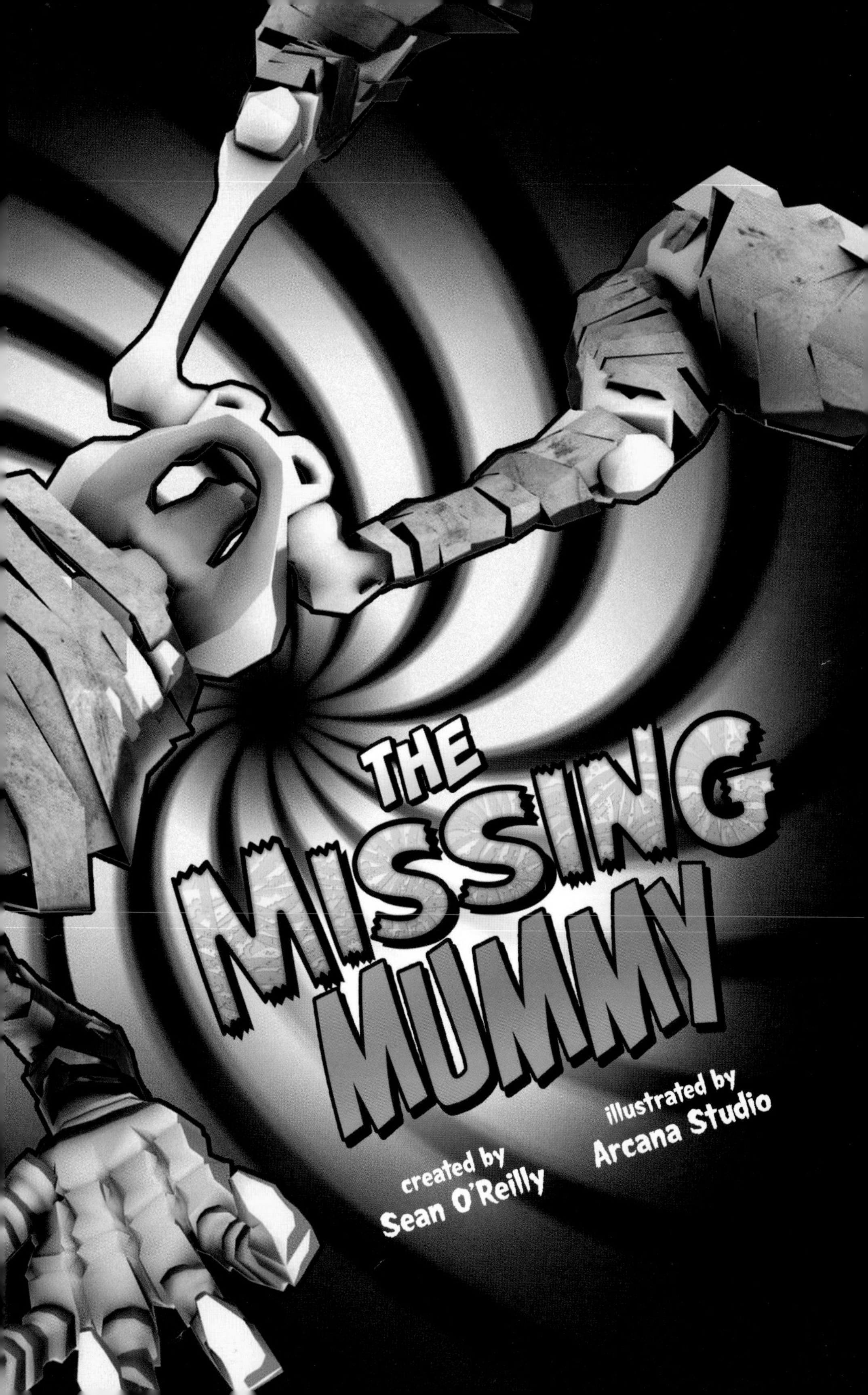
THE MISSING MUMMY
created by
Sean O'Reilly
illustrated by
Arcana Studio

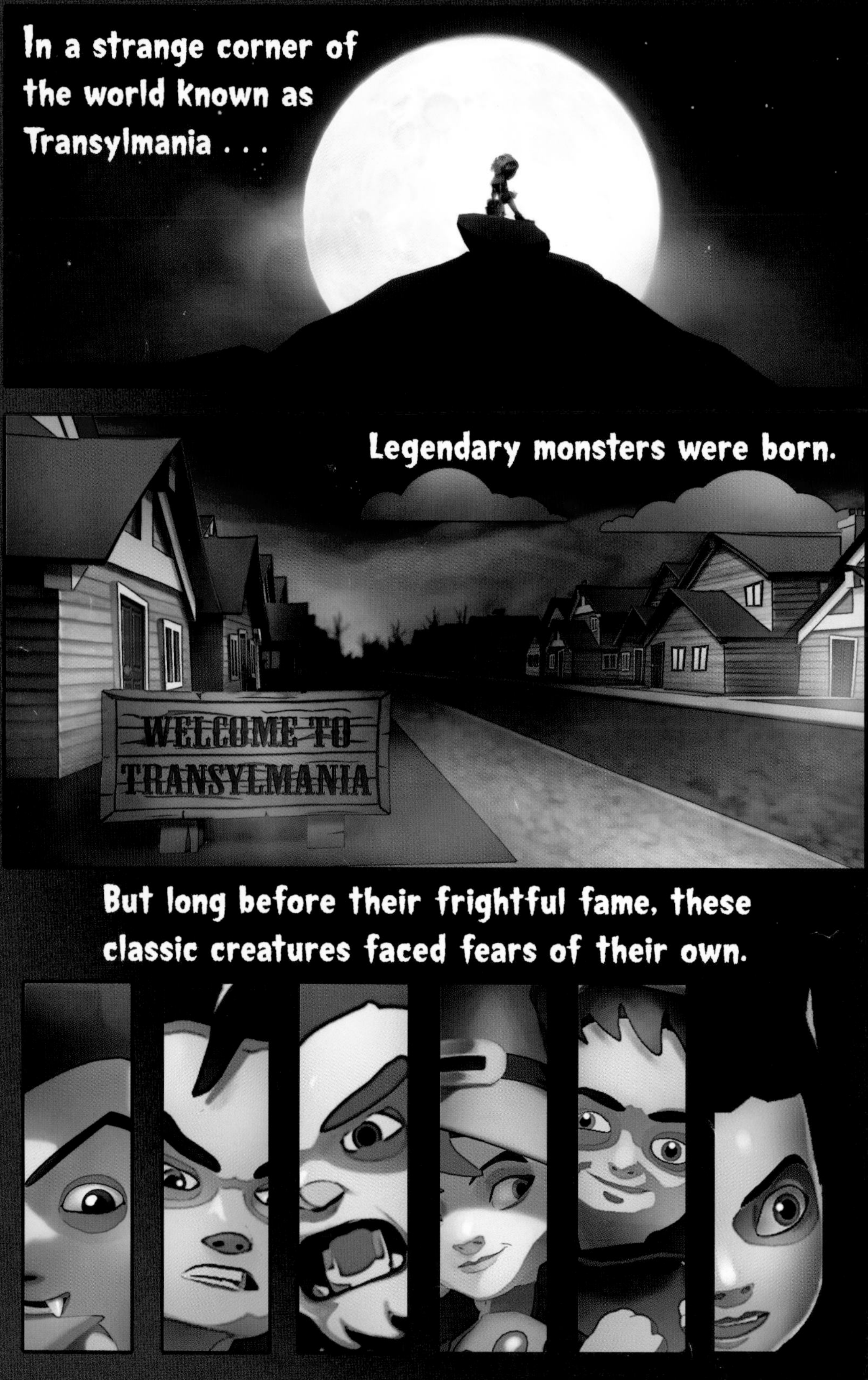
In a strange corner of the world known as Transylmania . . .
Legendary monsters were born.
WELCOME TO TRANSYLMANIA
But long before their frightful fame, these classic creatures faced fears of their own.

To take on terrifying teachers and homework horrors, they formed the most fearsome friendship on Earth . . .

Mighty Mighty MONSTERS

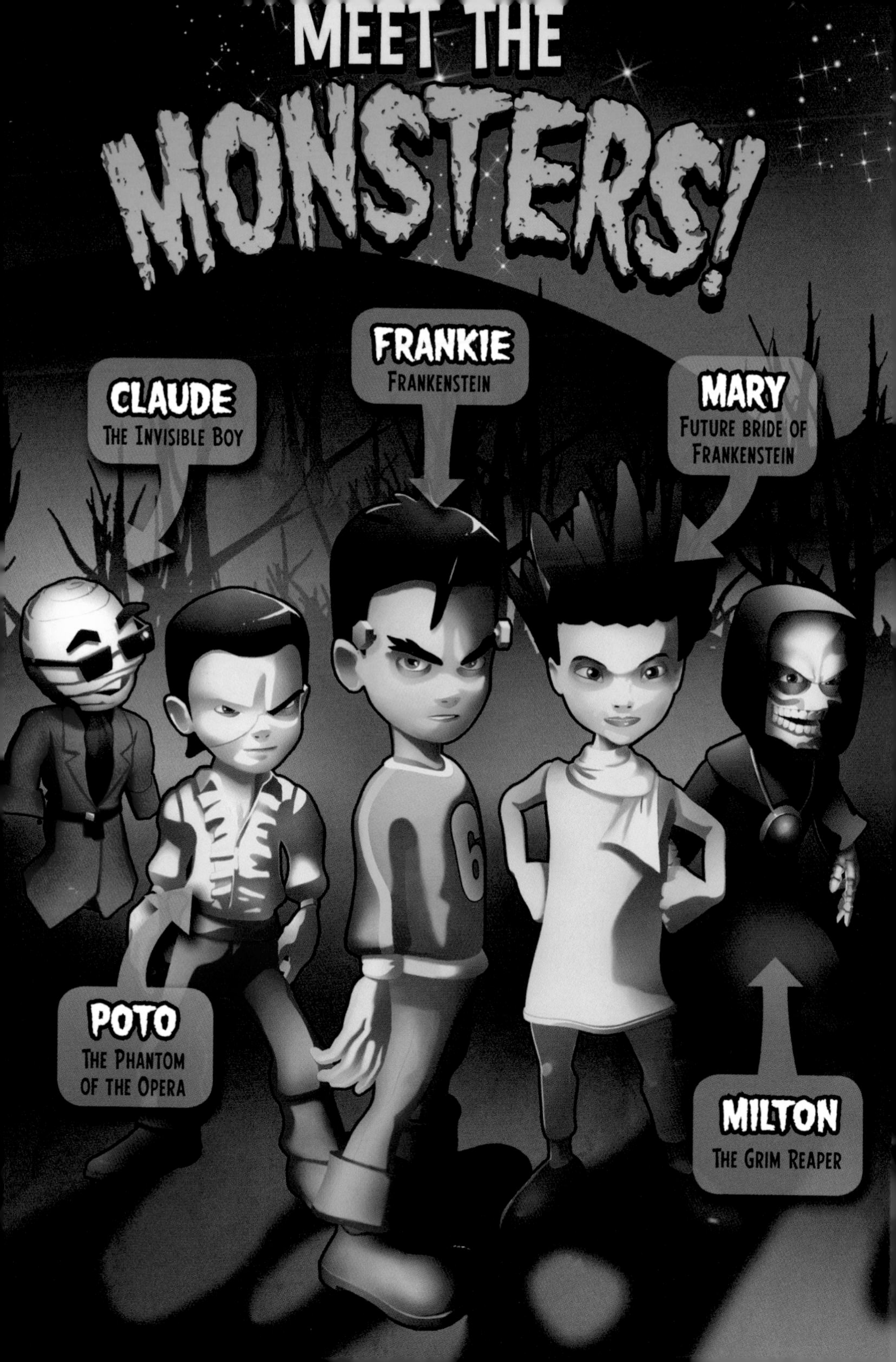
MEET THE
MONSTERS!
CLAUDE
THE INVISIBLE BOY
FRANKIE
FRANKENSTEIN
MARY
FUTURE BRIDE OF FRANKENSTEIN
POTO
THE PHANTOM OF THE OPERA
MILTON
THE GRIM REAPER

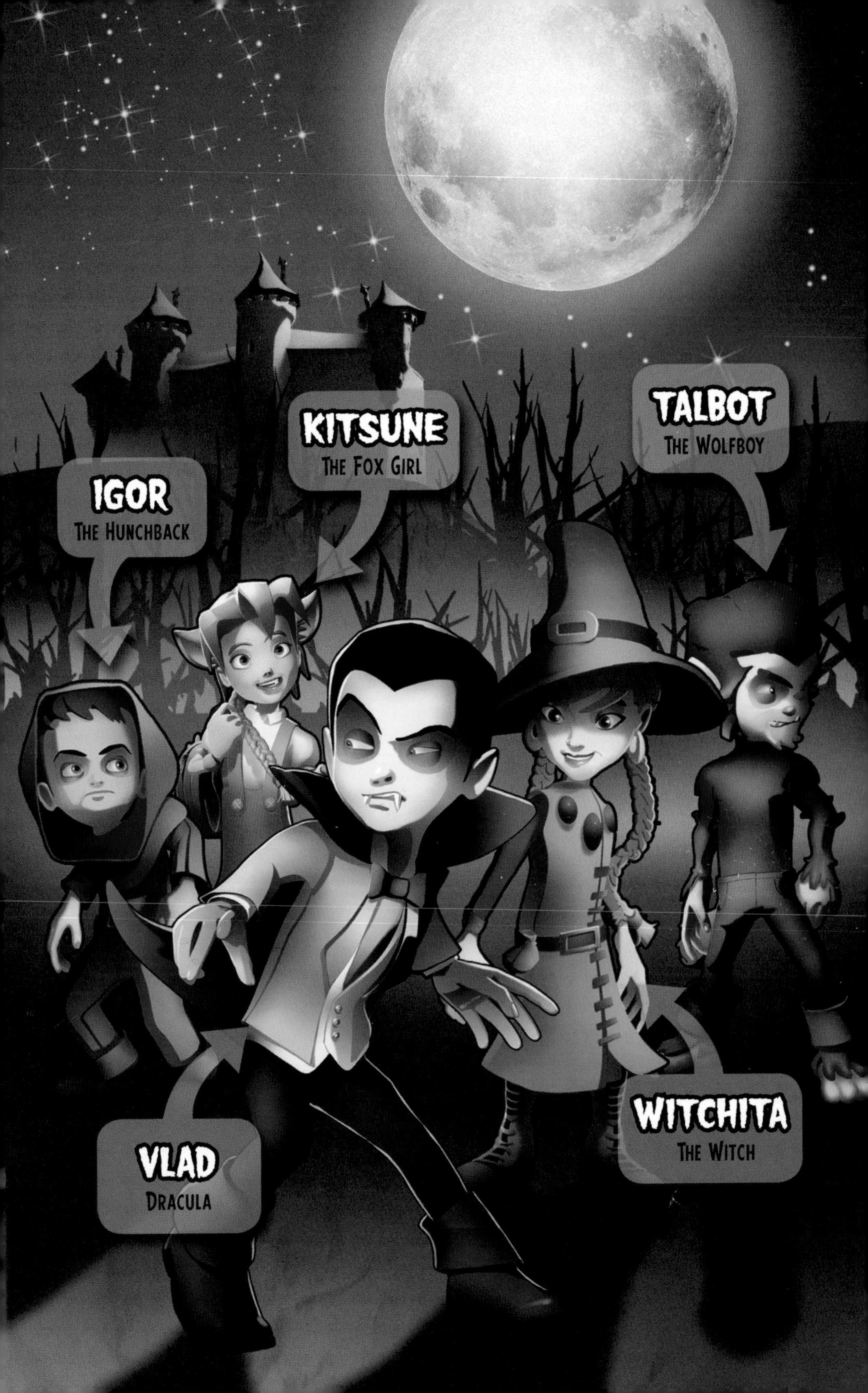
KITSUNE
THE FOX GIRL
TALBOT
THE WOLFBOY
IGOR
THE HUNCHBACK
VLAD
DRACULA
WITCHITA
THE WITCH

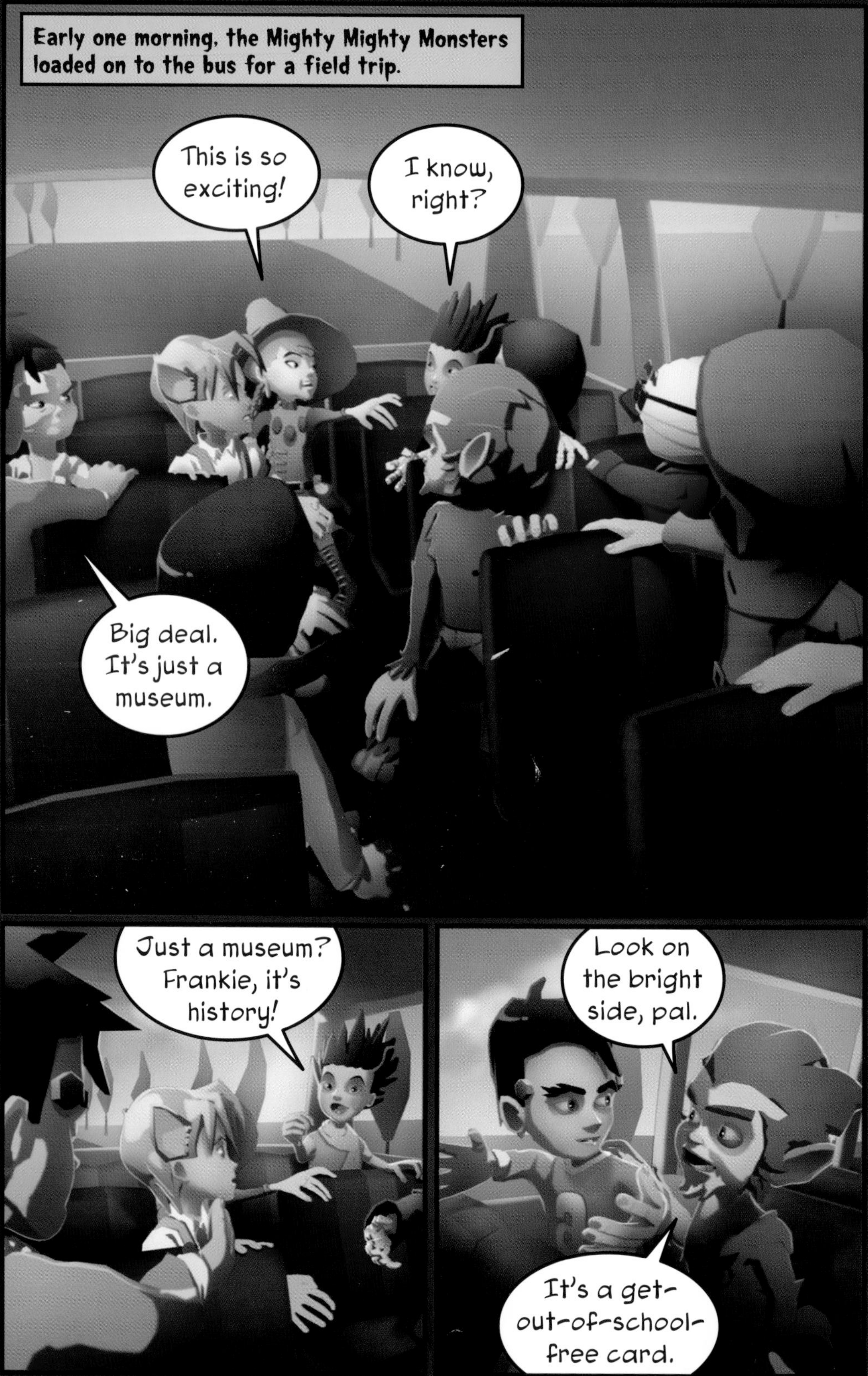
Early one morning, the Mighty Mighty Monsters loaded on to the bus for a field trip.
This is so exciting!
I know, right?
Big deal. It's just a museum.
Just a museum? Frankie, it's history!
Look on the bright side, pal.
It's a get-out-of-school-free card.

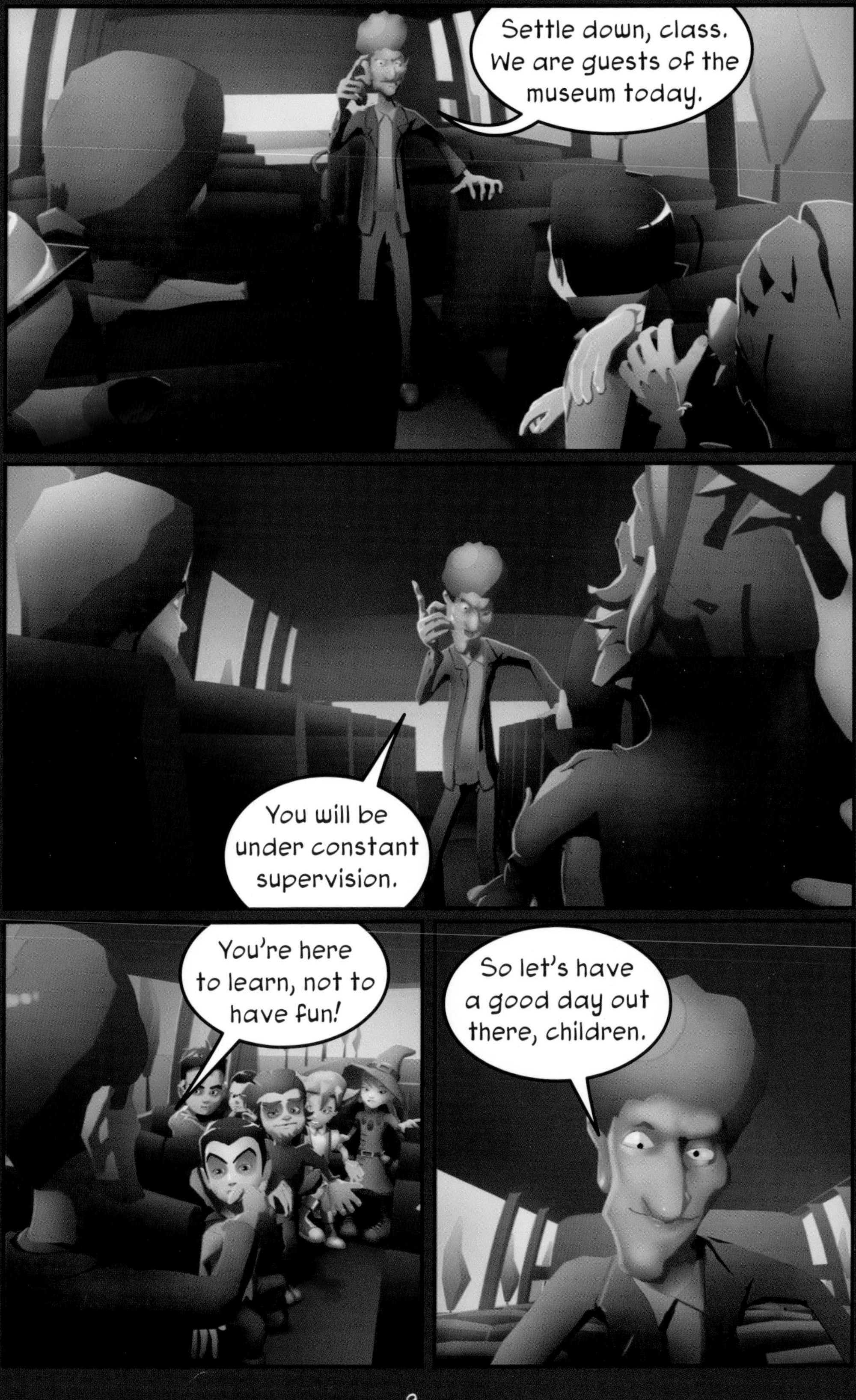
Settle down, class. We are guests of the museum today.
You will be under constant supervision.
You're here to learn, not to have fun!
So let's have a good day out there, children.

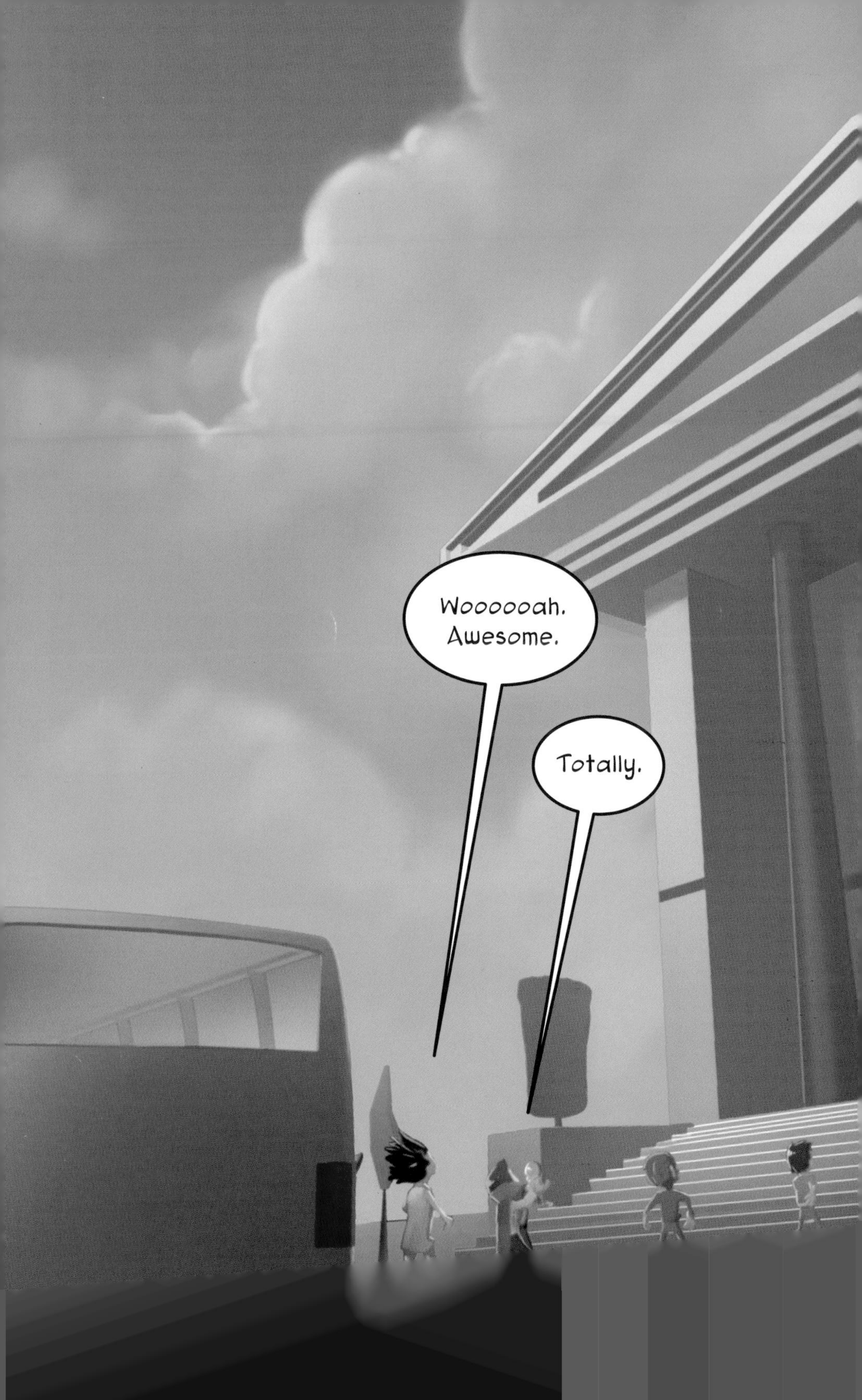
Woooooah. Awesome.
Totally.

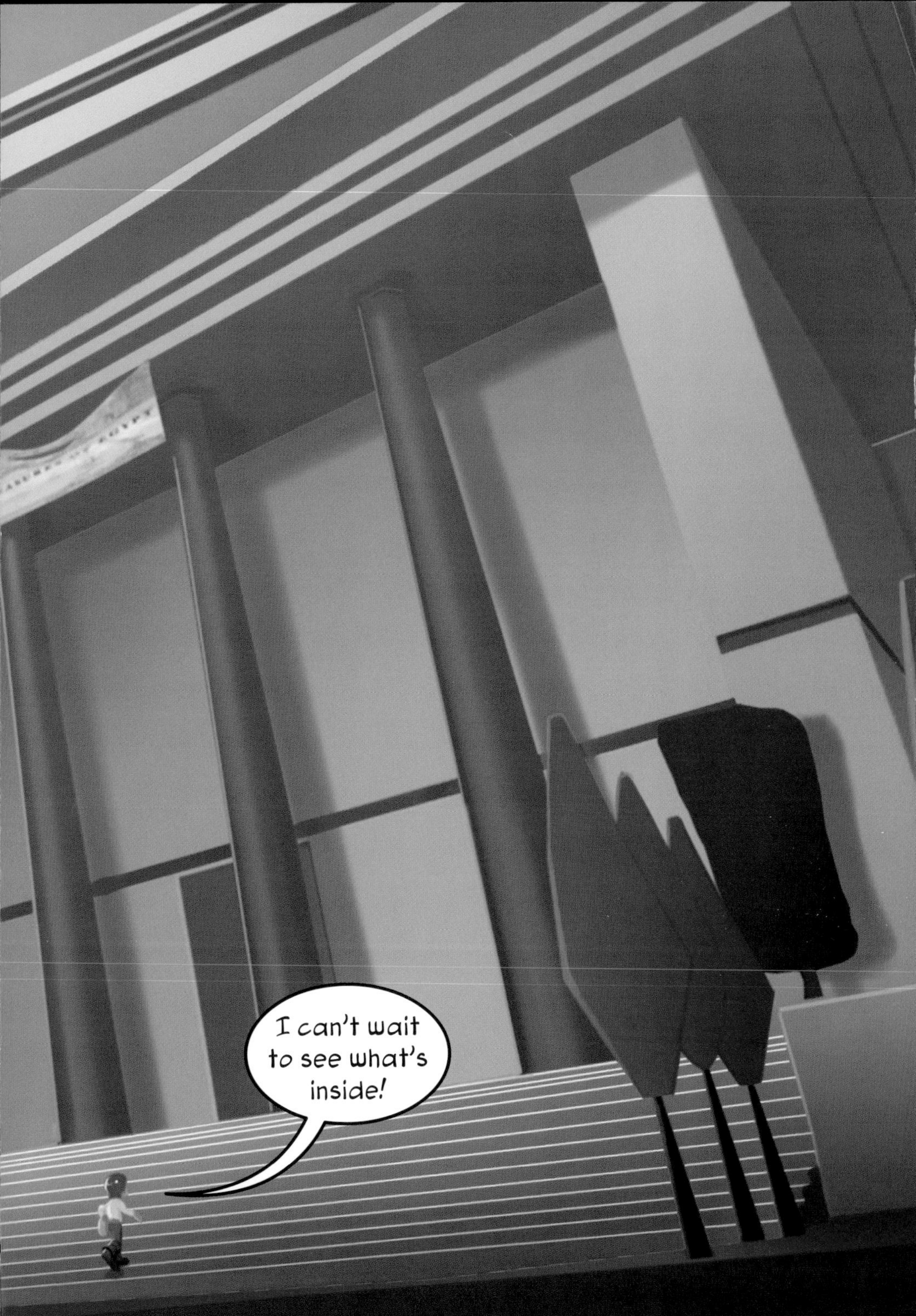
I can't wait to see what's inside!

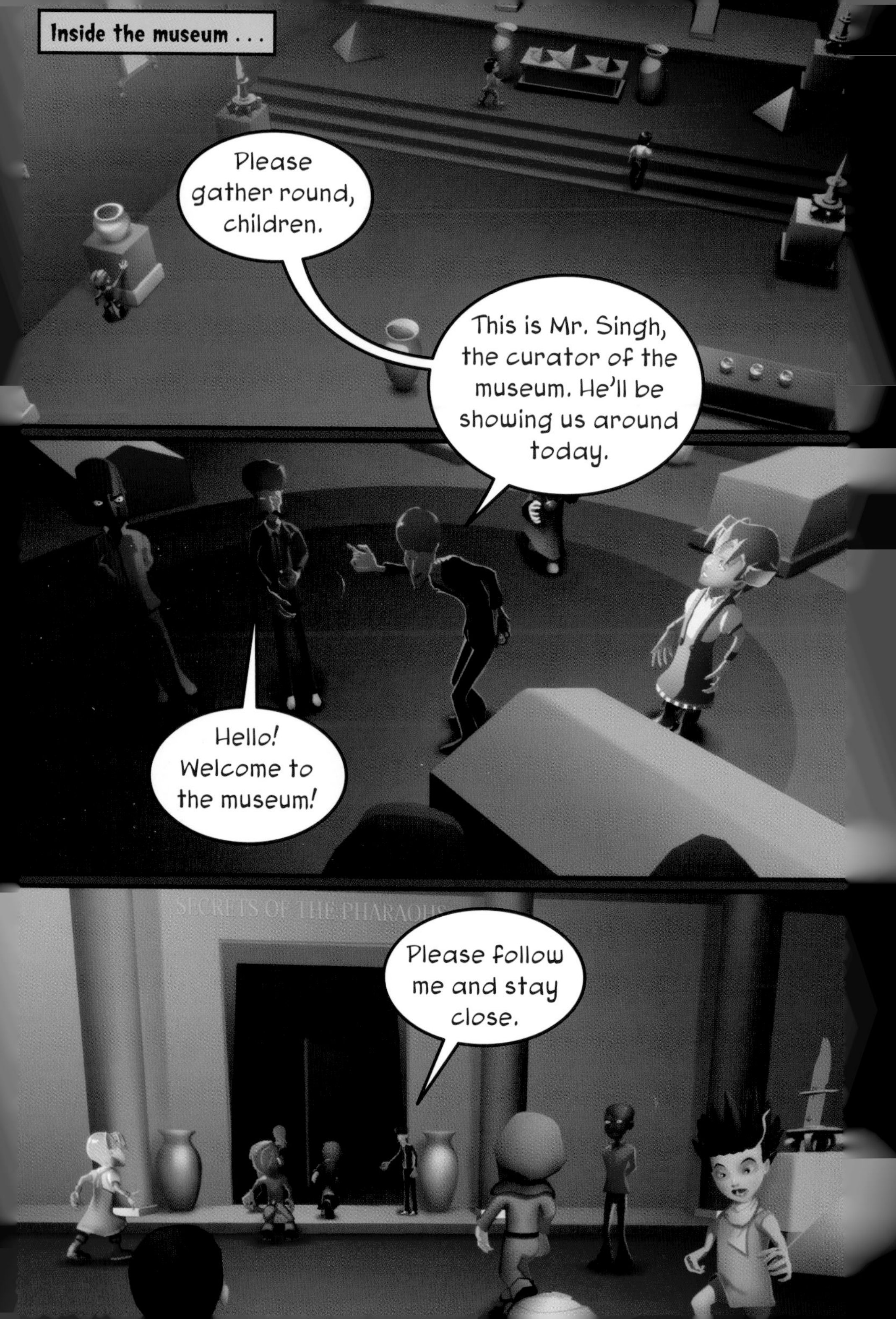

Inside the museum . . .
Please gather round, children.
This is Mr. Singh, the curator of the museum. He'll be showing us around today.
Hello! Welcome to the museum!
SECRETS OF THE PHARAOHS
Please follow me and stay close.

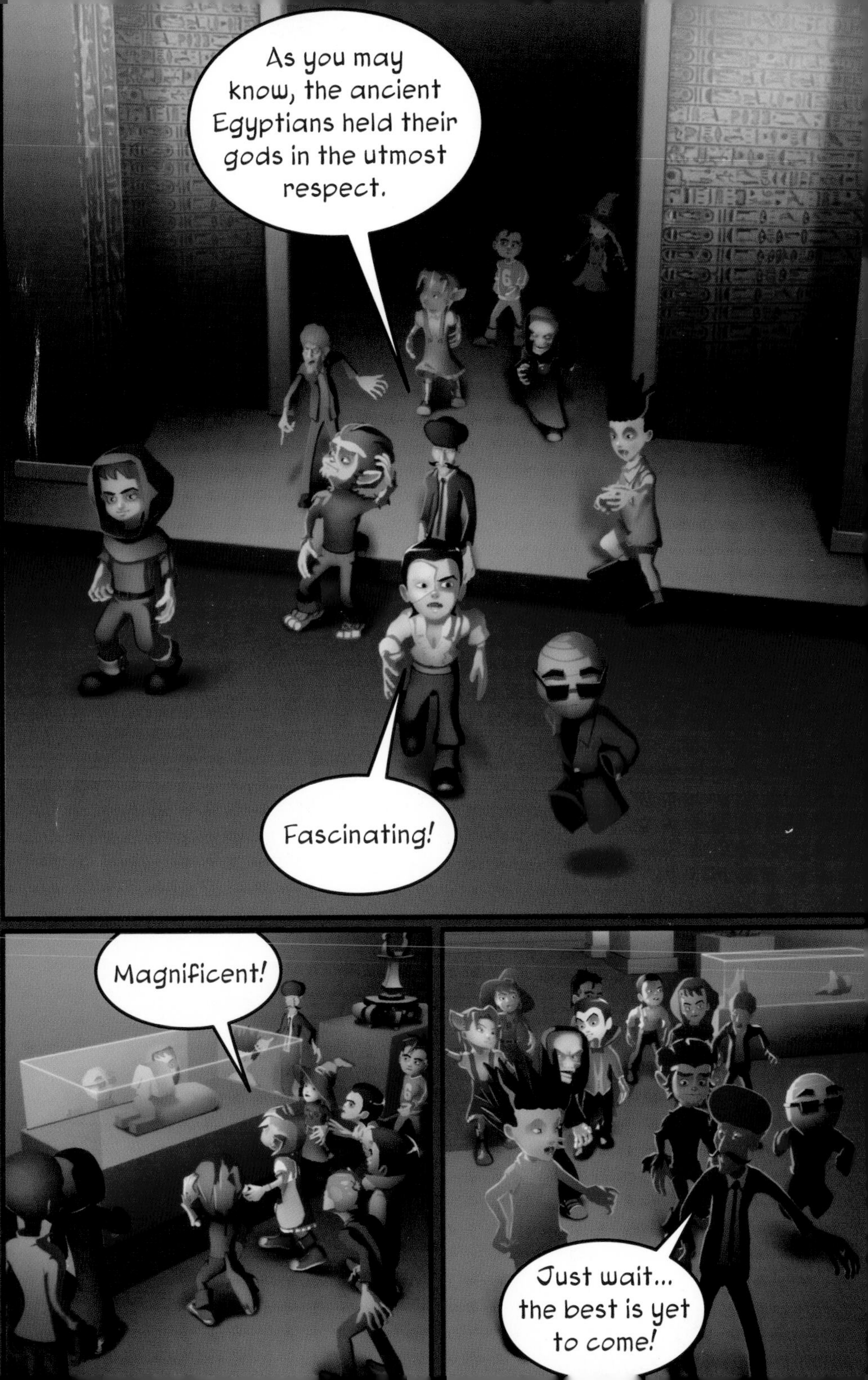

As you may know, the ancient Egyptians held their gods in the utmost respect.
Fascinating!
Magnificent!
Just wait... the best is yet to come!

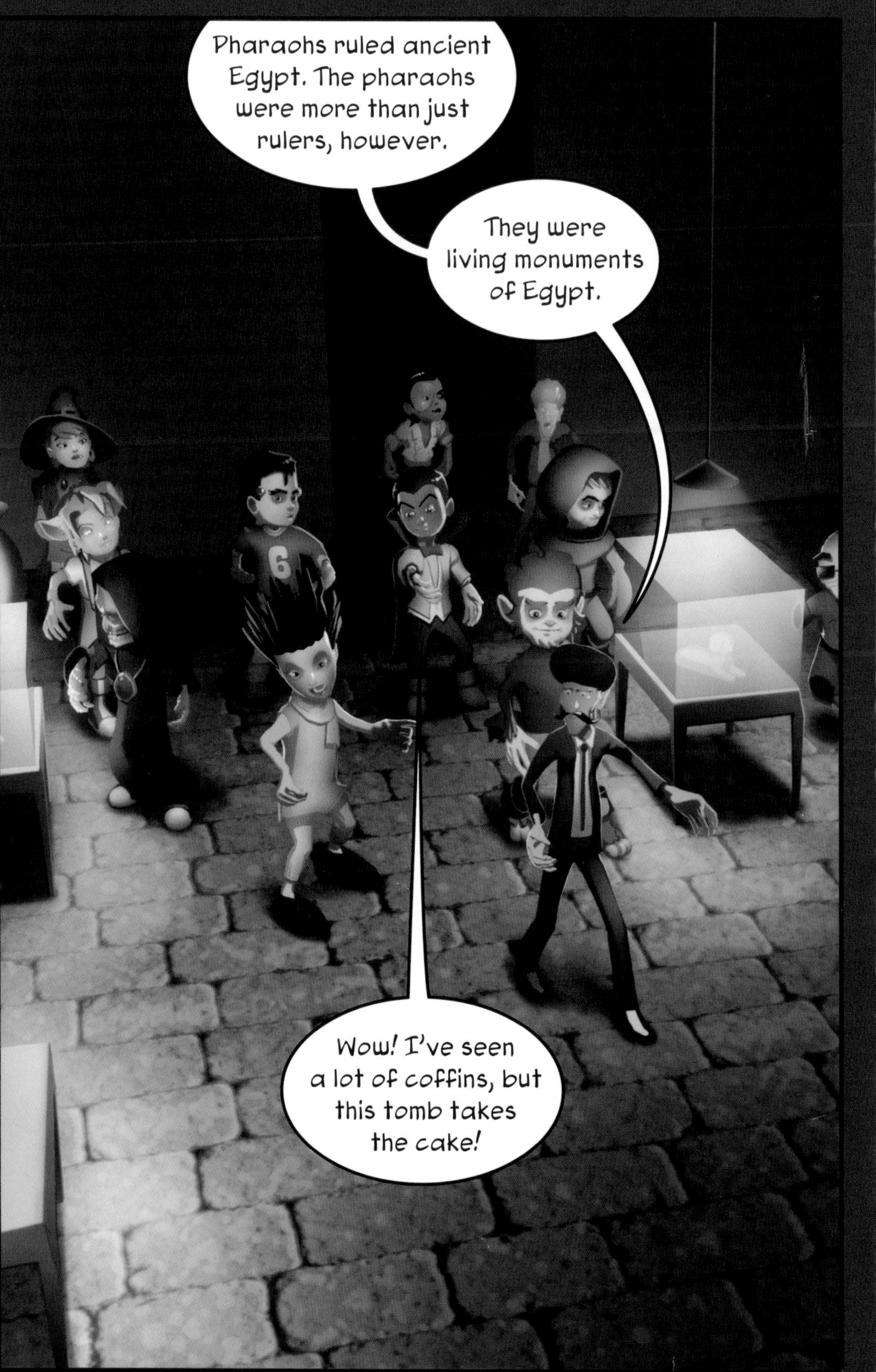
Pharaohs ruled ancient Egypt. The pharaohs were more than just rulers, however.
They were living monuments of Egypt.
Wow! I've seen a lot of coffins, but this tomb takes the cake!

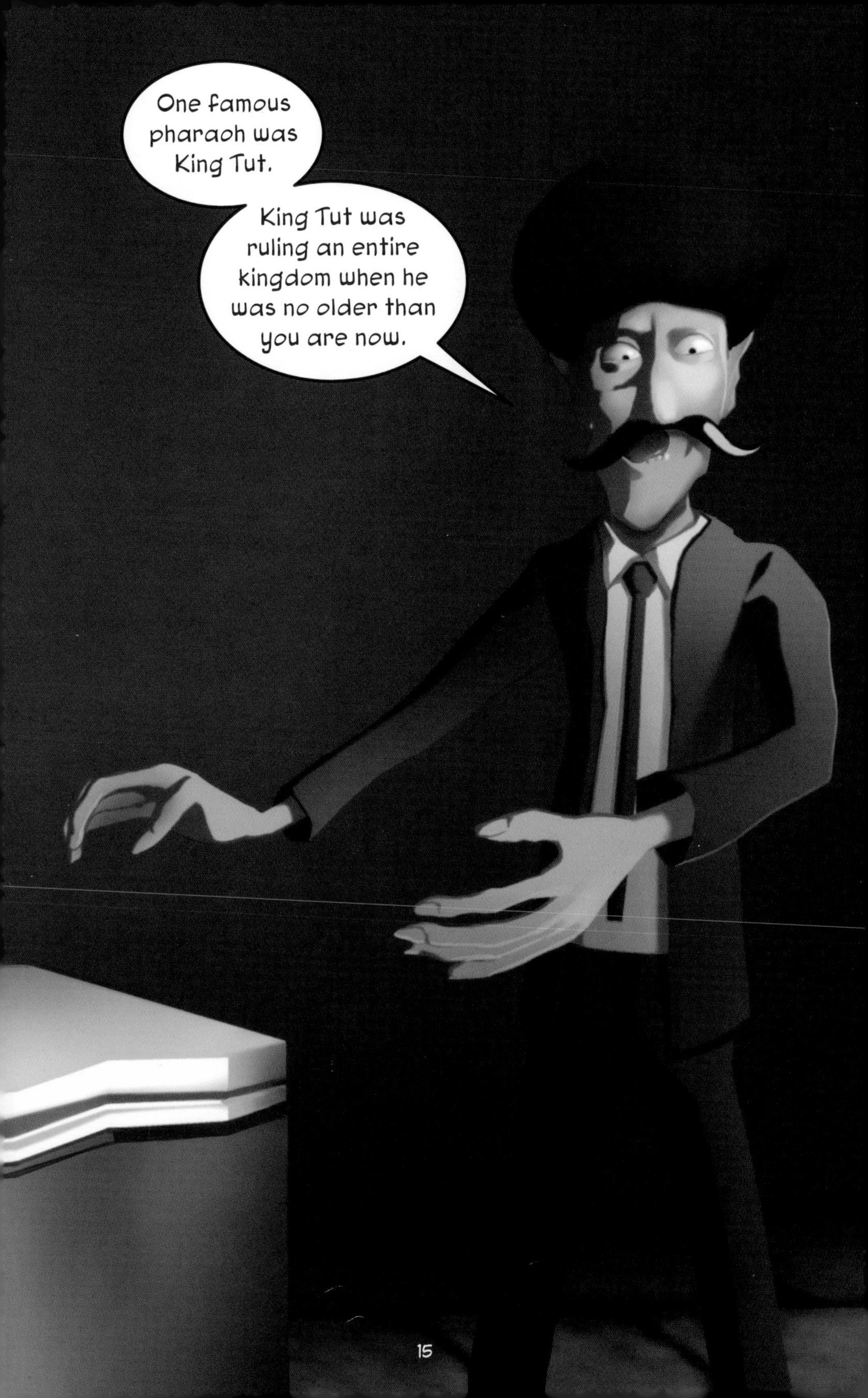
One famous pharaoh was King Tut.
King Tut was ruling an entire kingdom when he was no older than you are now.

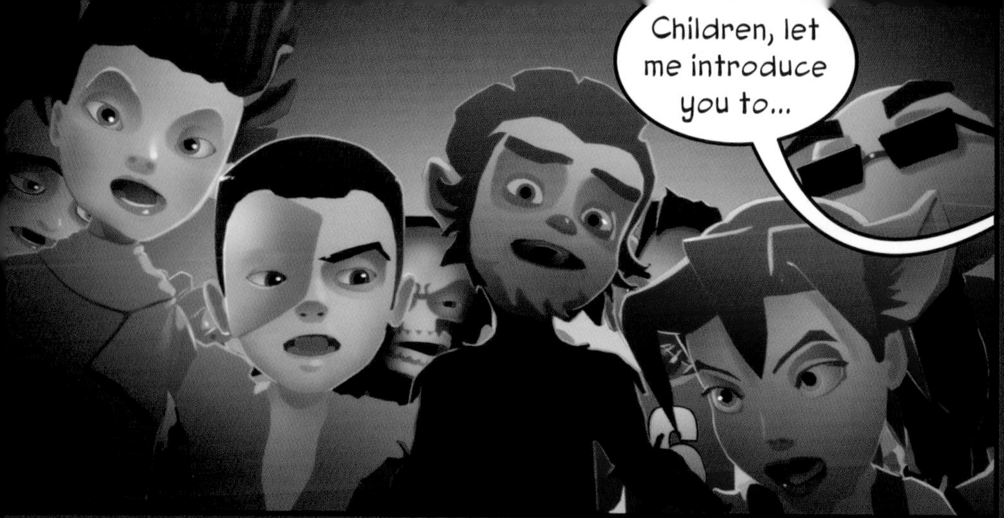
Children, let me introduce you to...

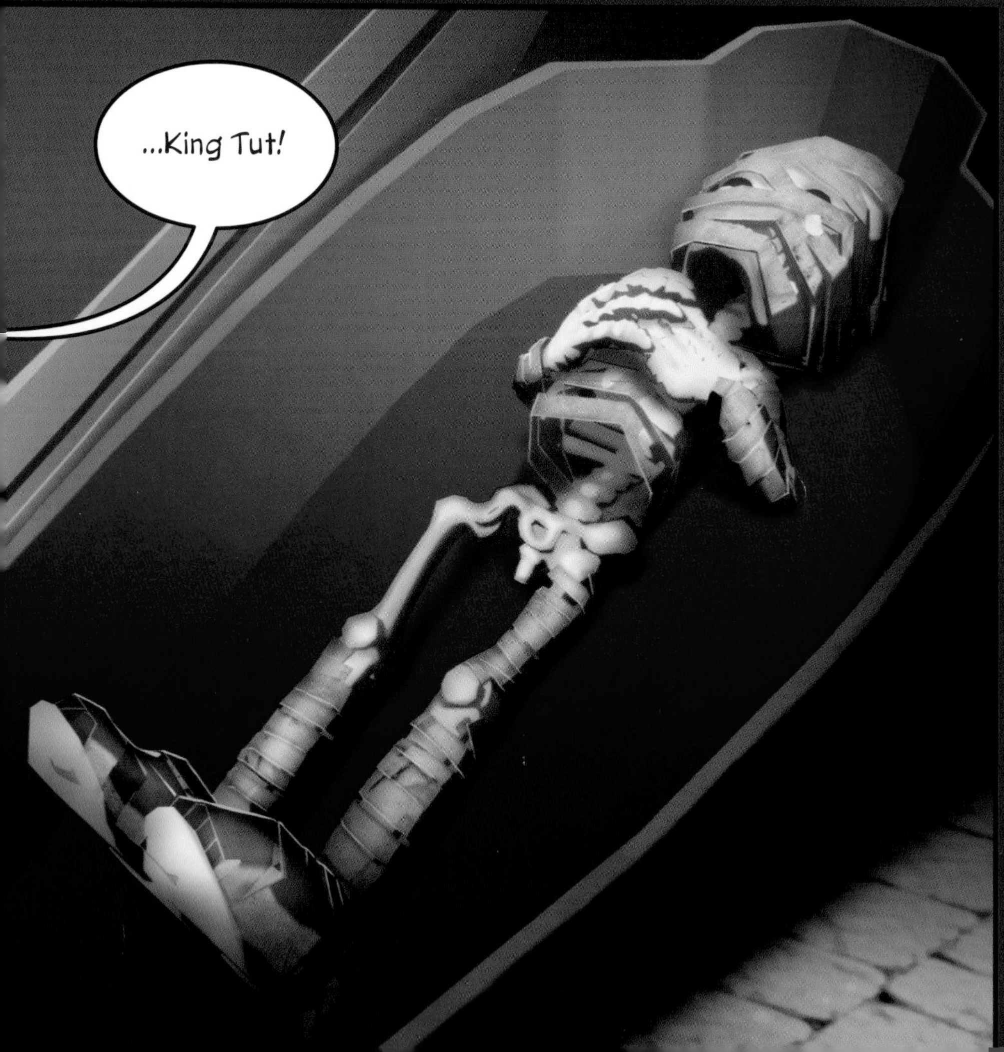
...King Tut!

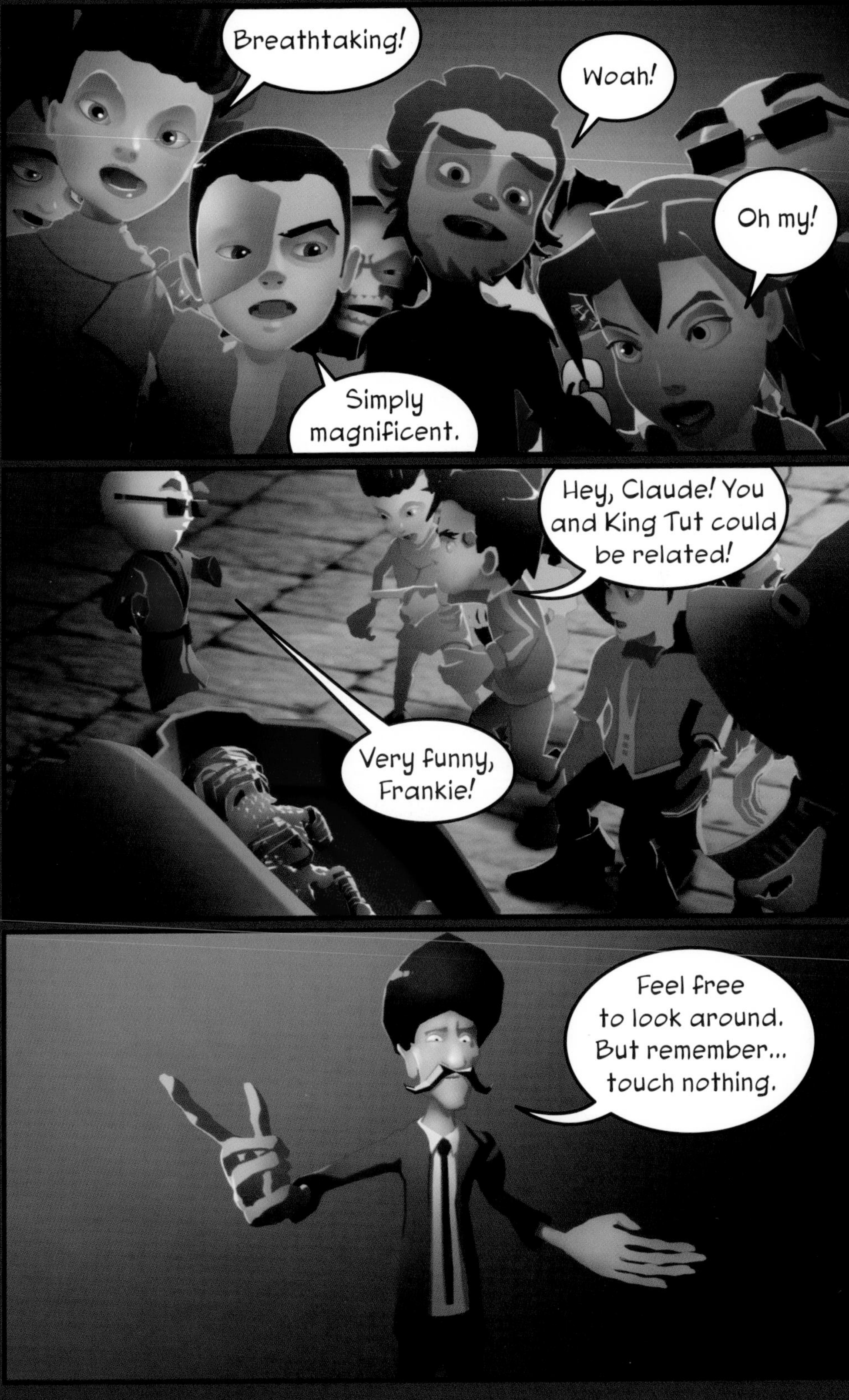

Breathtaking!
Woah!
Oh my!
Simply magnificent.
Hey, Claude! You and King Tut could be related!
Very funny, Frankie!
Feel free to look around. But remember... touch nothing.

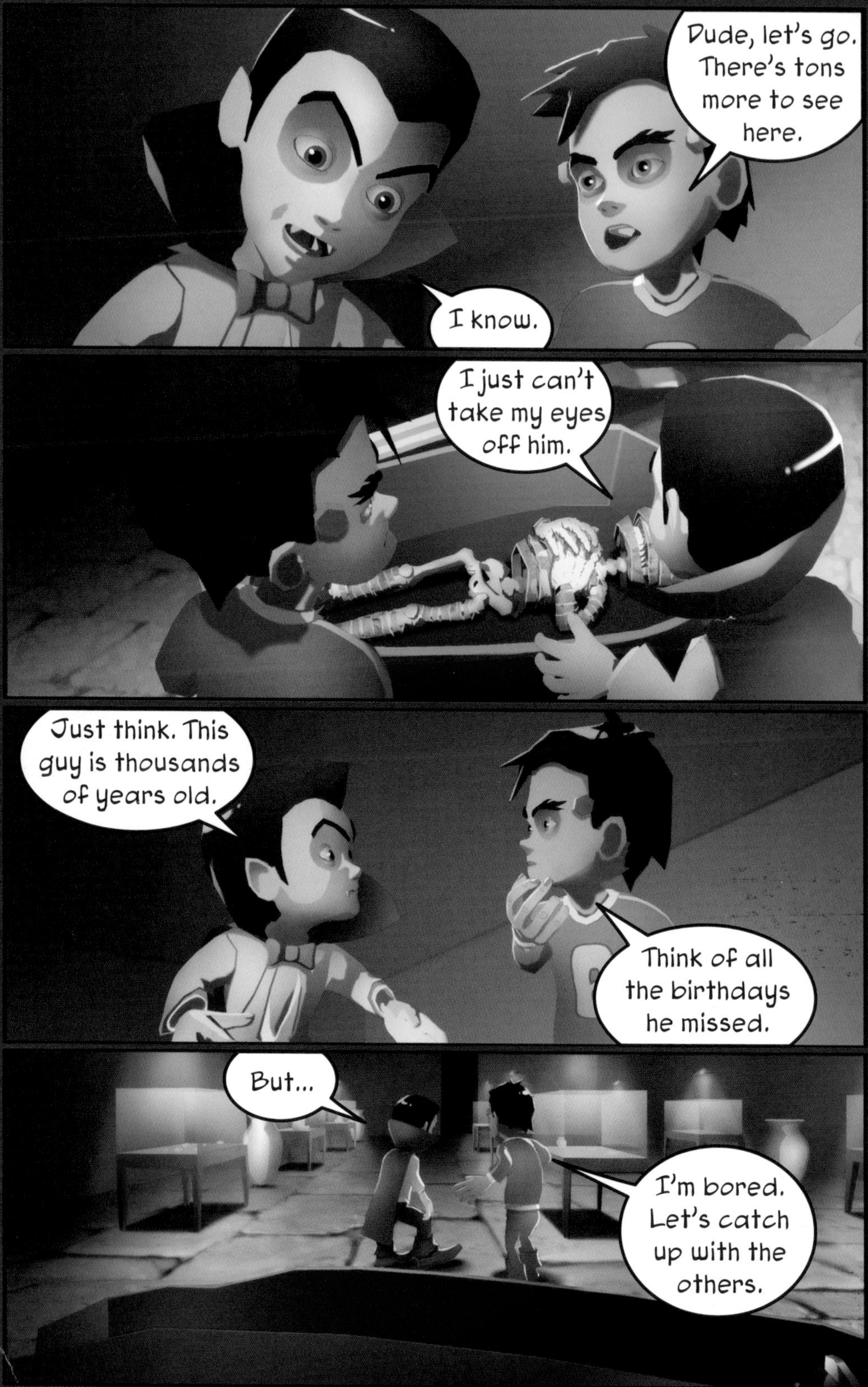
Dude, let's go. There's tons more to see here.
I know.
I just can't take my eyes off him.
Just think. This guy is thousands of years old.
Think of all the birthdays he missed.
But...
I'm bored. Let's catch up with the others.

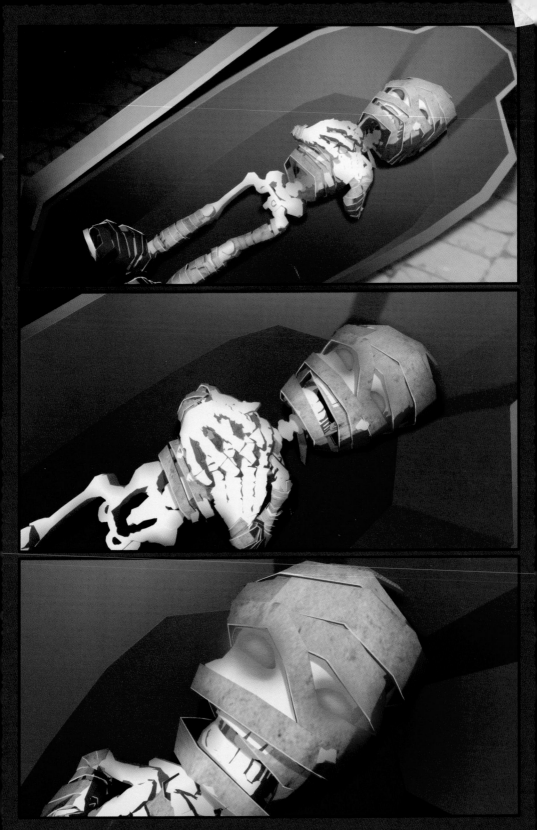

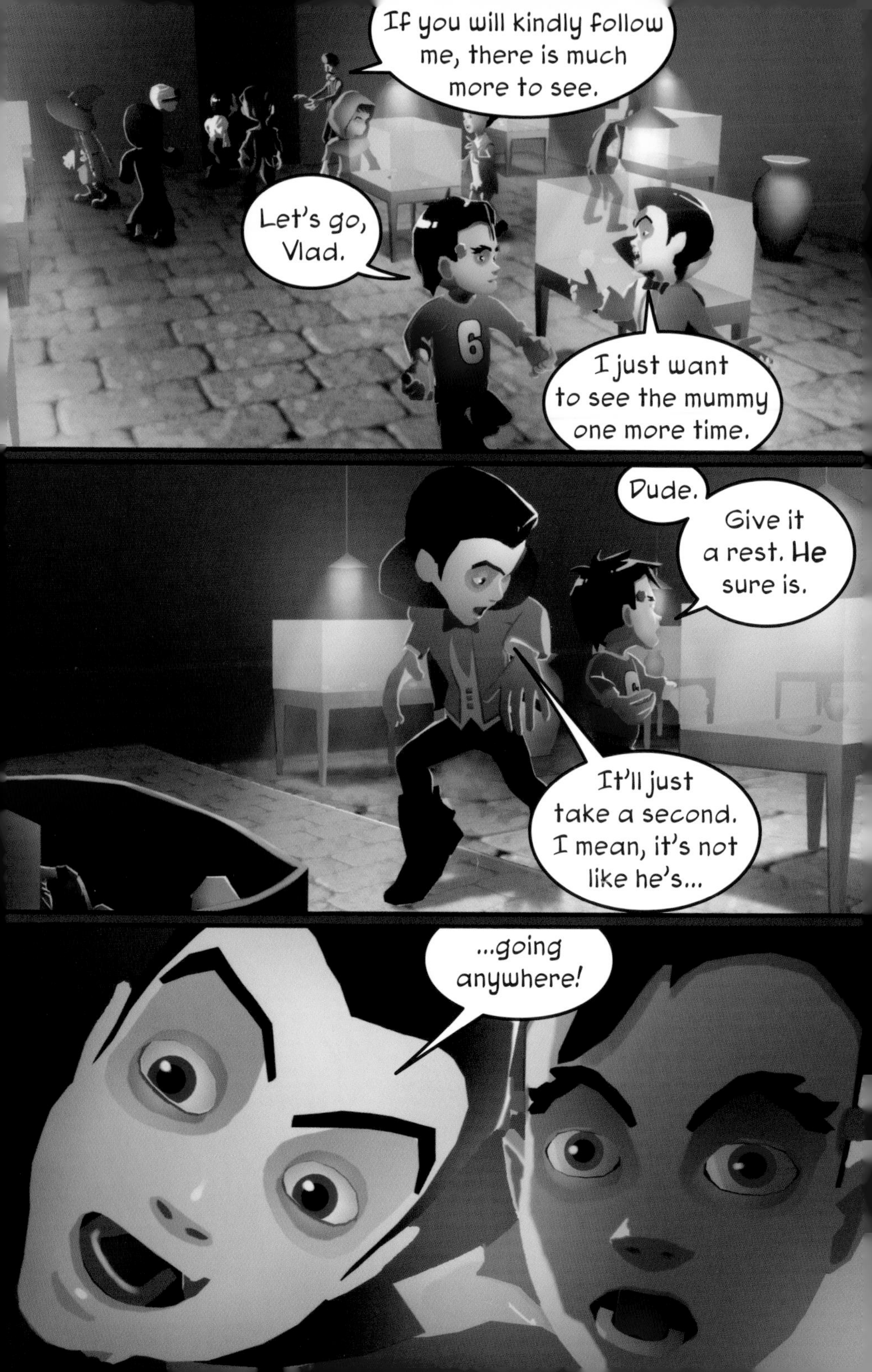

If you will kindly follow me, there is much more to see.
Let's go, Vlad.
I just want to see the mummy one more time.
Dude.
Give it a rest. He sure is.
It'll just take a second. I mean, it's not like he's...
...going anywhere!

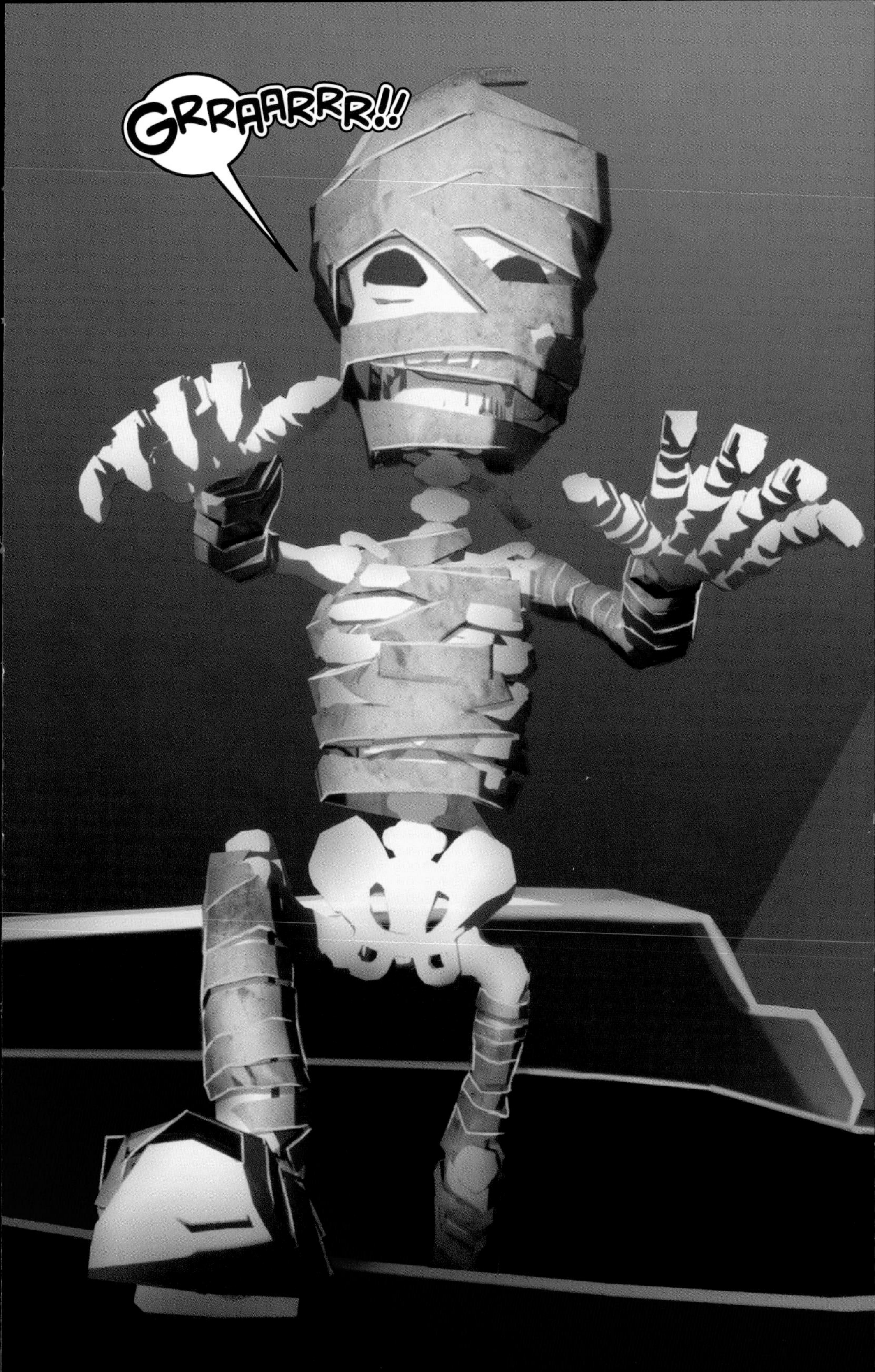
GRRAARRR!!

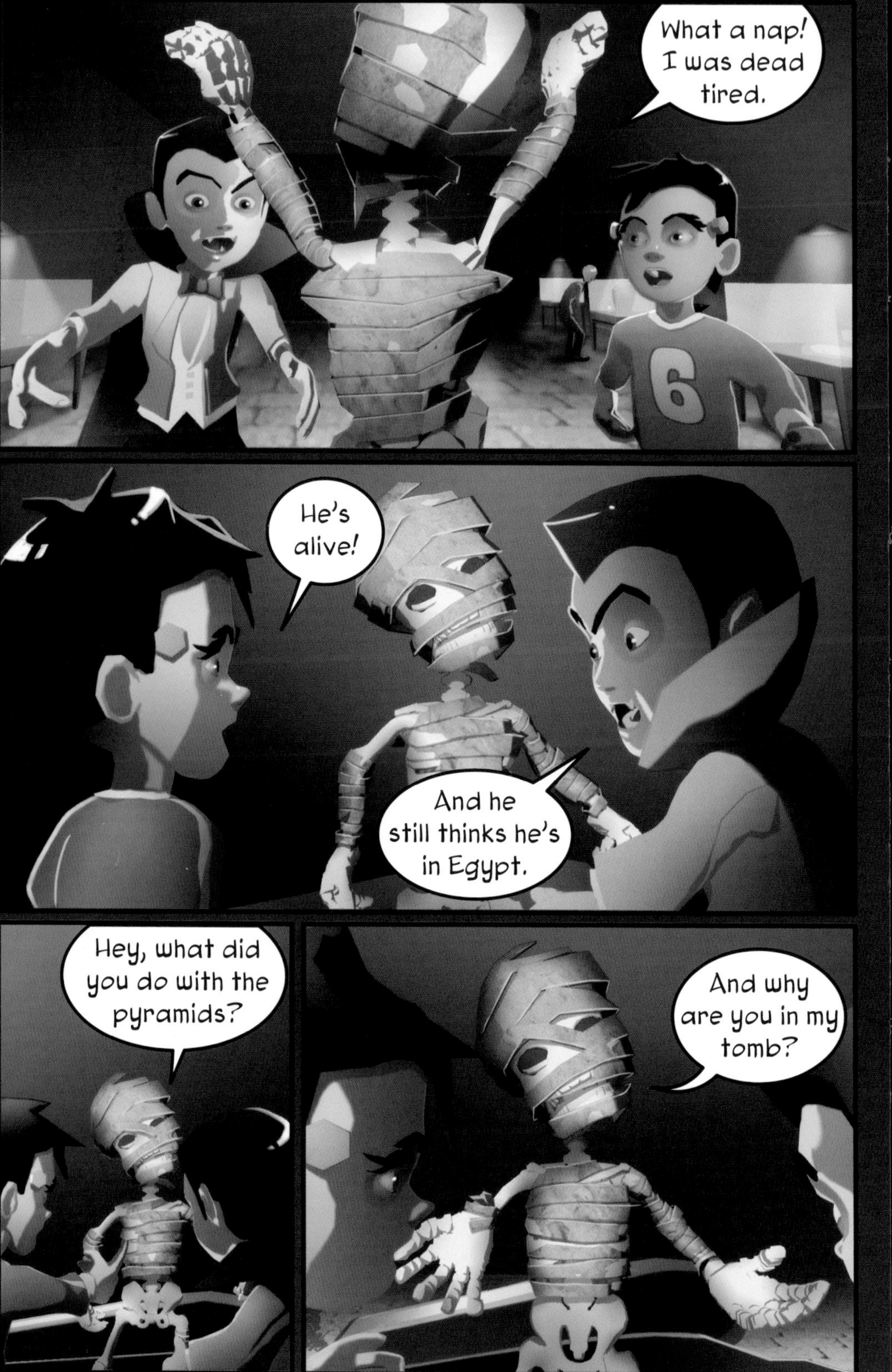
What a nap! I was dead tired.
He's alive!
And he still thinks he's in Egypt.
Hey, what did you do with the pyramids?
And why are you in my tomb?

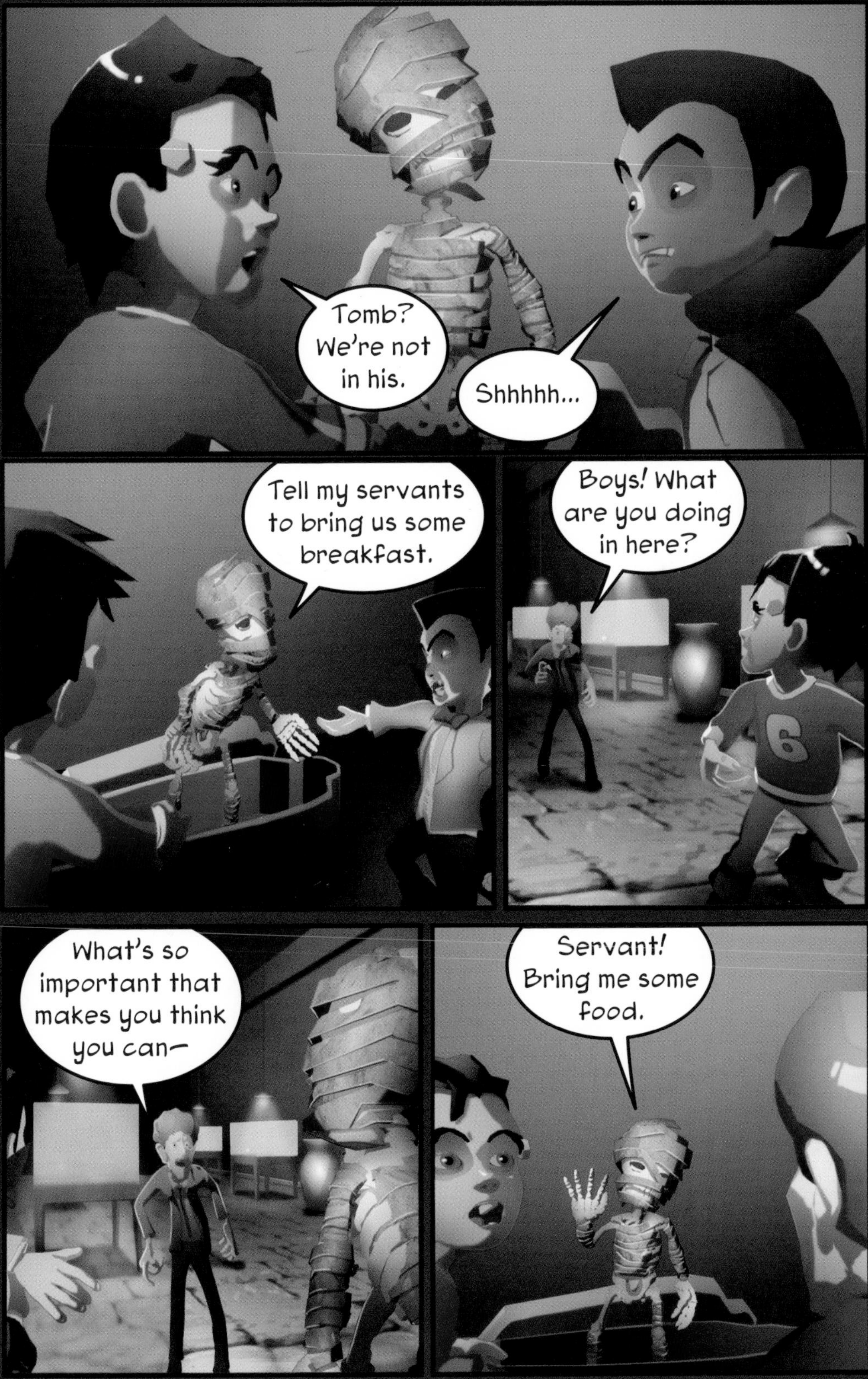
Tomb? We're not in his.
Shhhhh...
Tell my servants to bring us some breakfast.
Boys! What are you doing in here?
What's so important that makes you think you can—
Servant! Bring me some food.

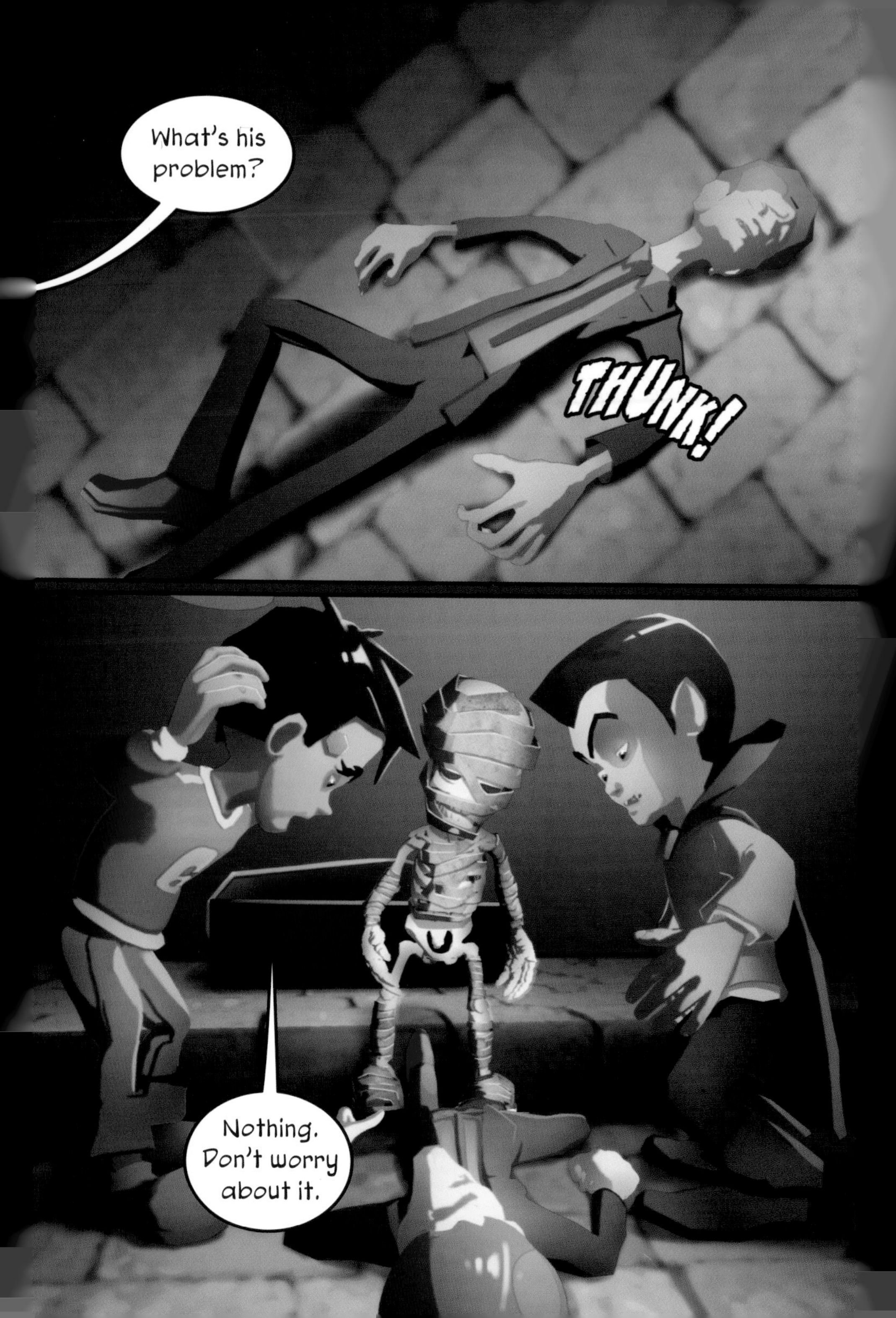
What's his problem?
THUNK!
Nothing. Don't worry about it.

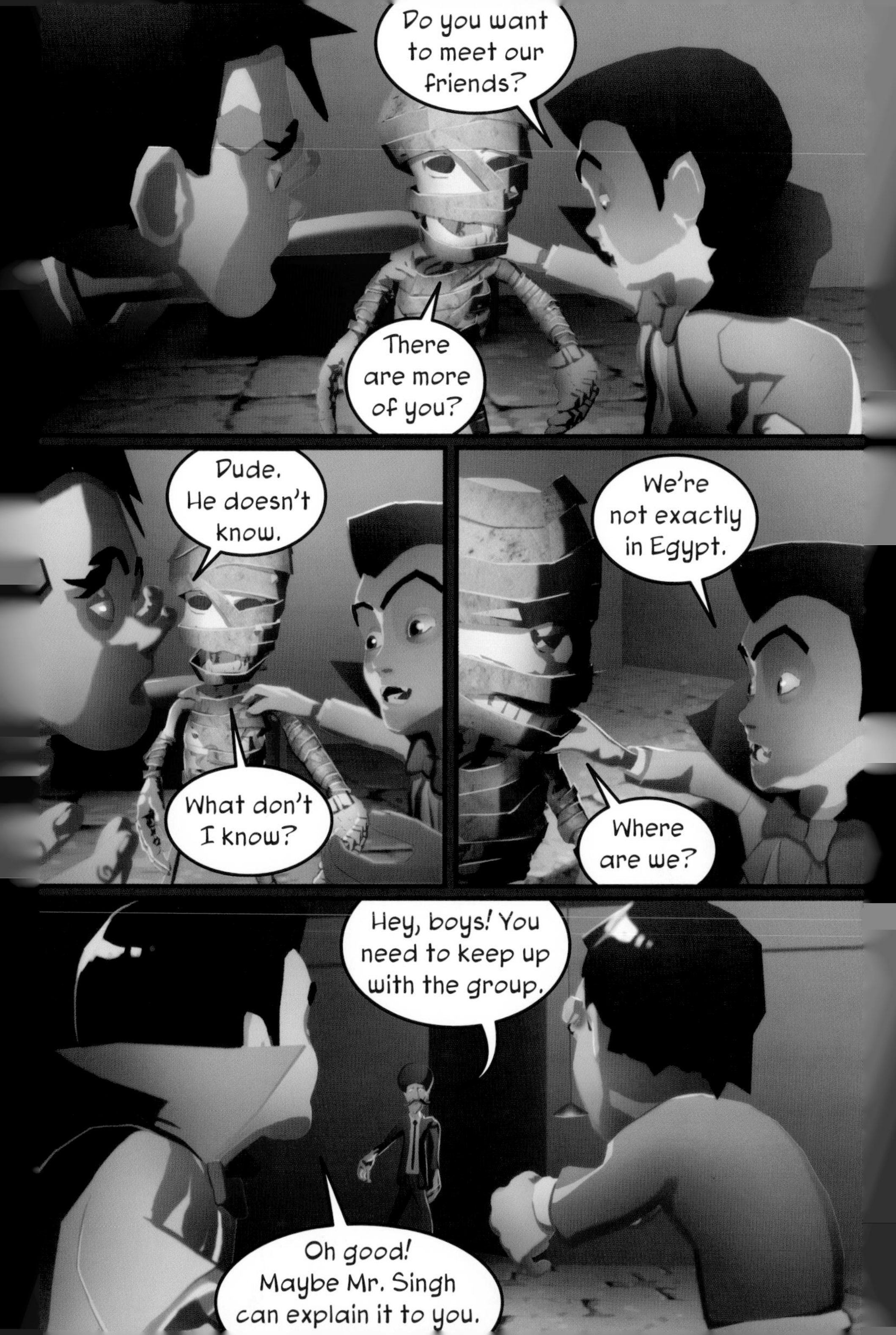
Do you want to meet our friends?
There are more of you?
Dude. He doesn't know.
What don't I know?
We're not exactly in Egypt.
Where are we?
Hey, boys! You need to keep up with the group.
Oh good! Maybe Mr. Singh can explain it to you.

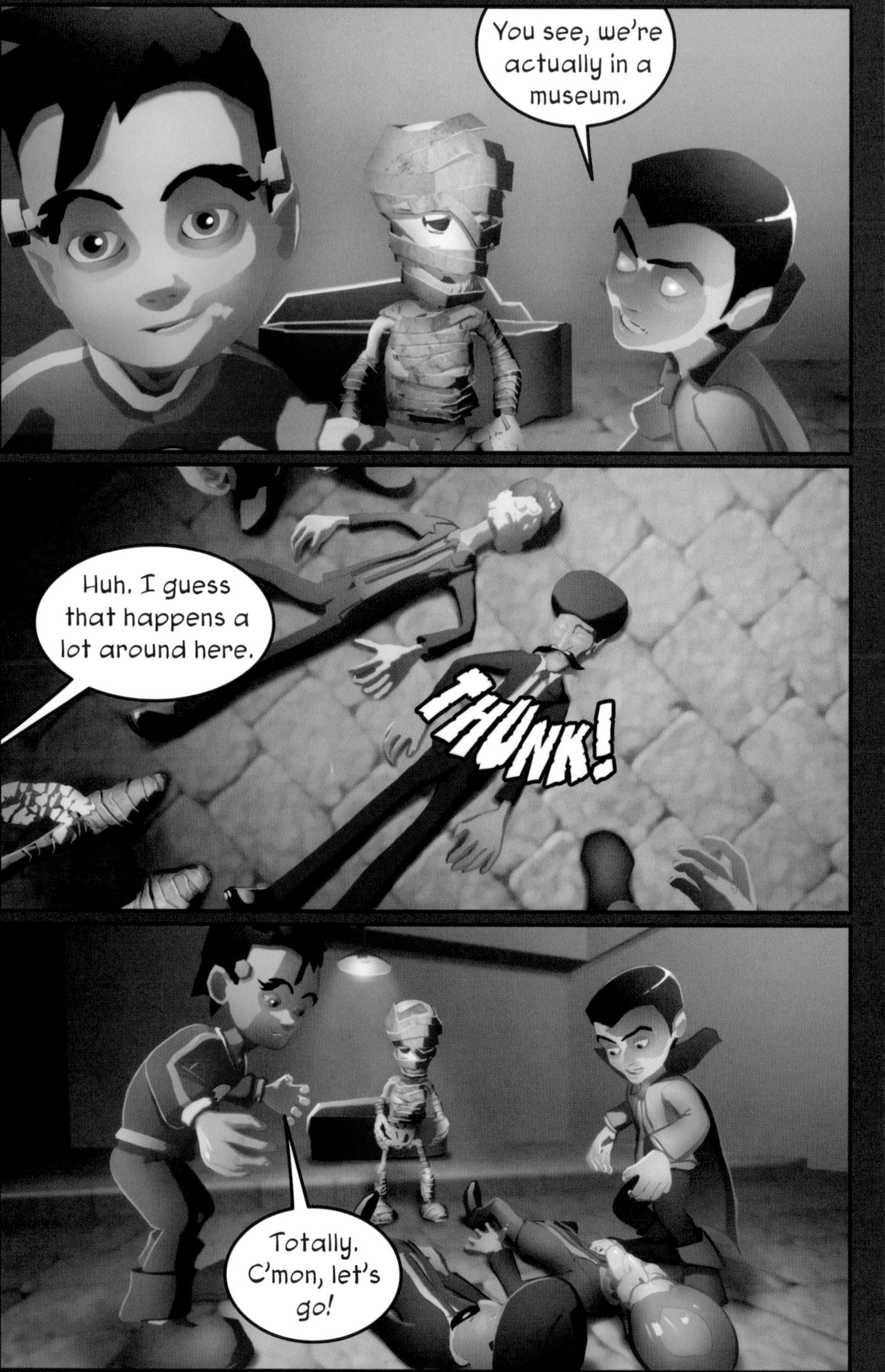
You see, we're actually in a museum.
Huh. I guess that happens a lot around here.
THUNK!
Totally. C'mon, let's go!

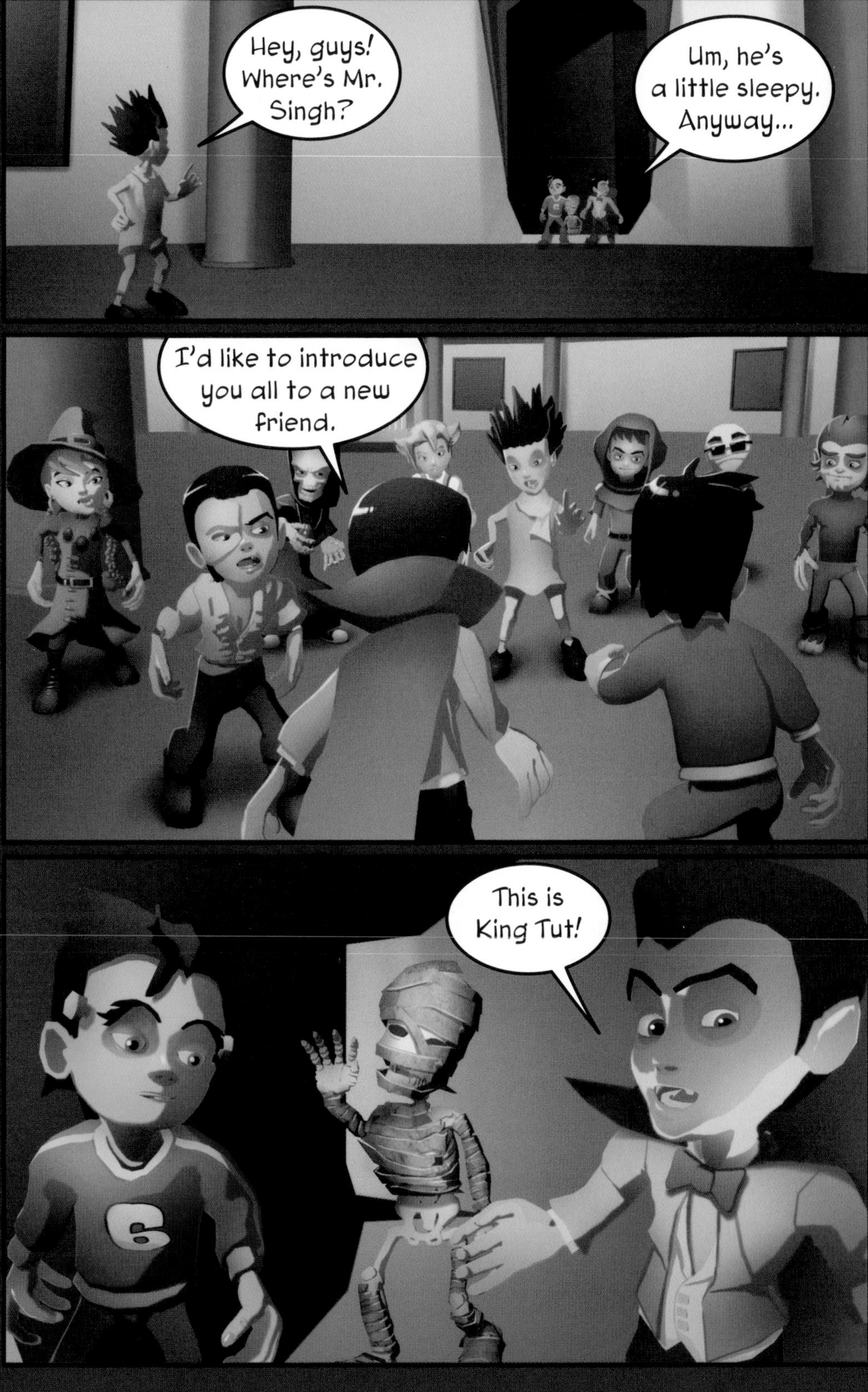
Hey, guys! Where's Mr. Singh?
Um, he's a little sleepy. Anyway...
I'd like to introduce you all to a new friend.
This is King Tut!

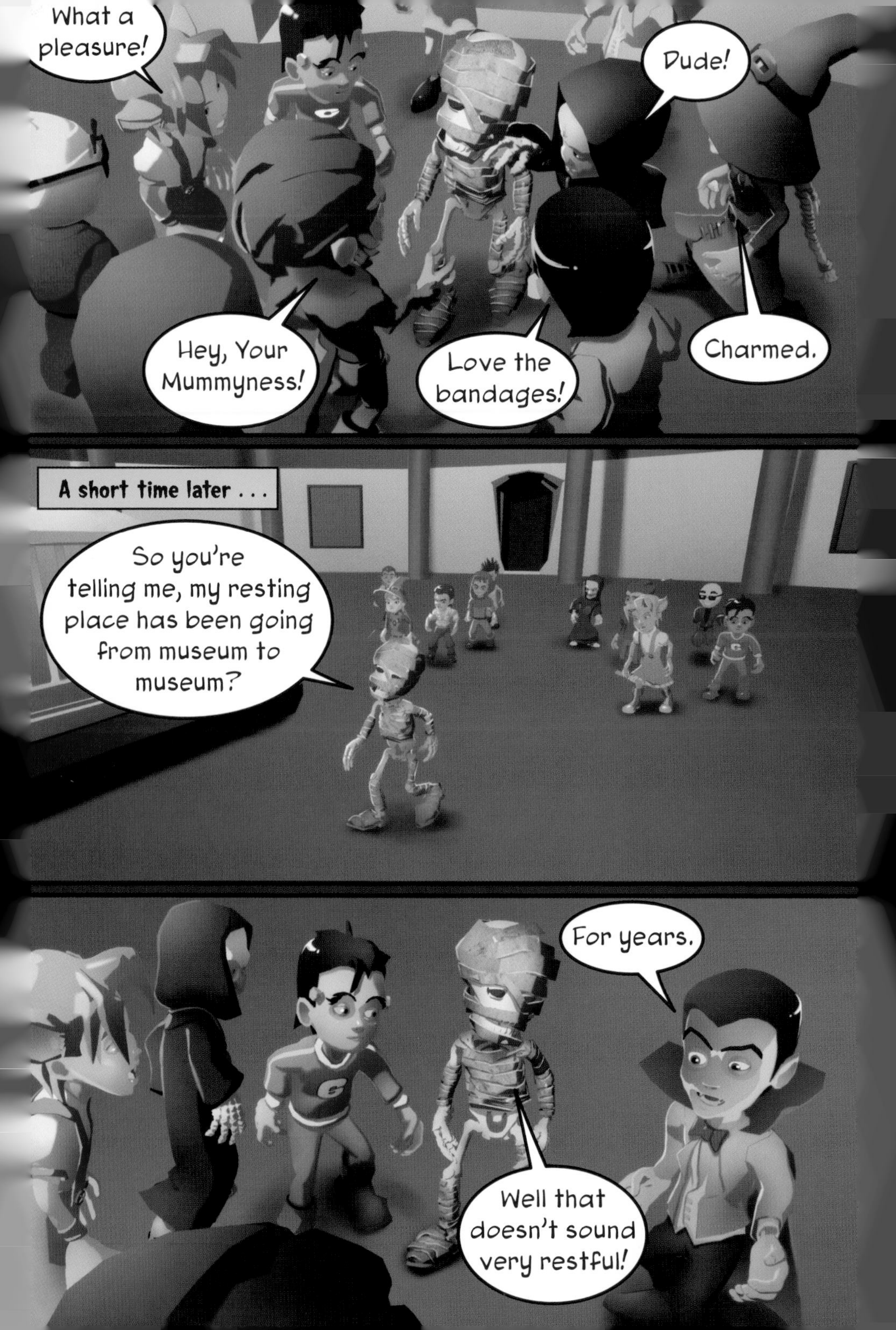
What a pleasure!
Dude!
Hey, Your Mummyness!
Love the bandages!
Charmed.
A short time later . . .
So you're telling me, my resting place has been going from museum to museum?
For years.
Well that doesn't sound very restful!

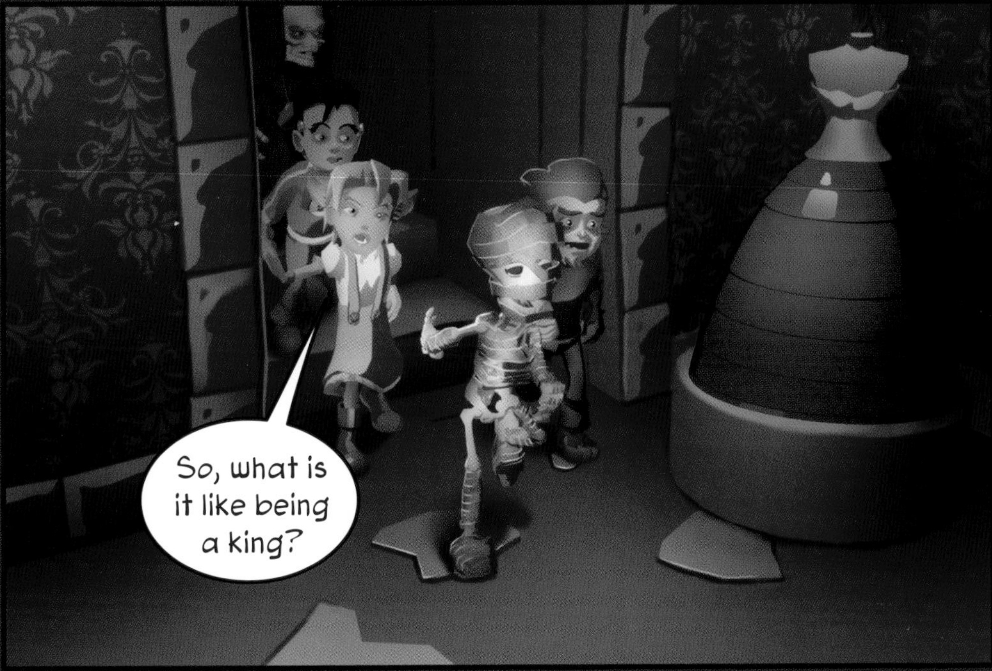
So, what is it like being a king?

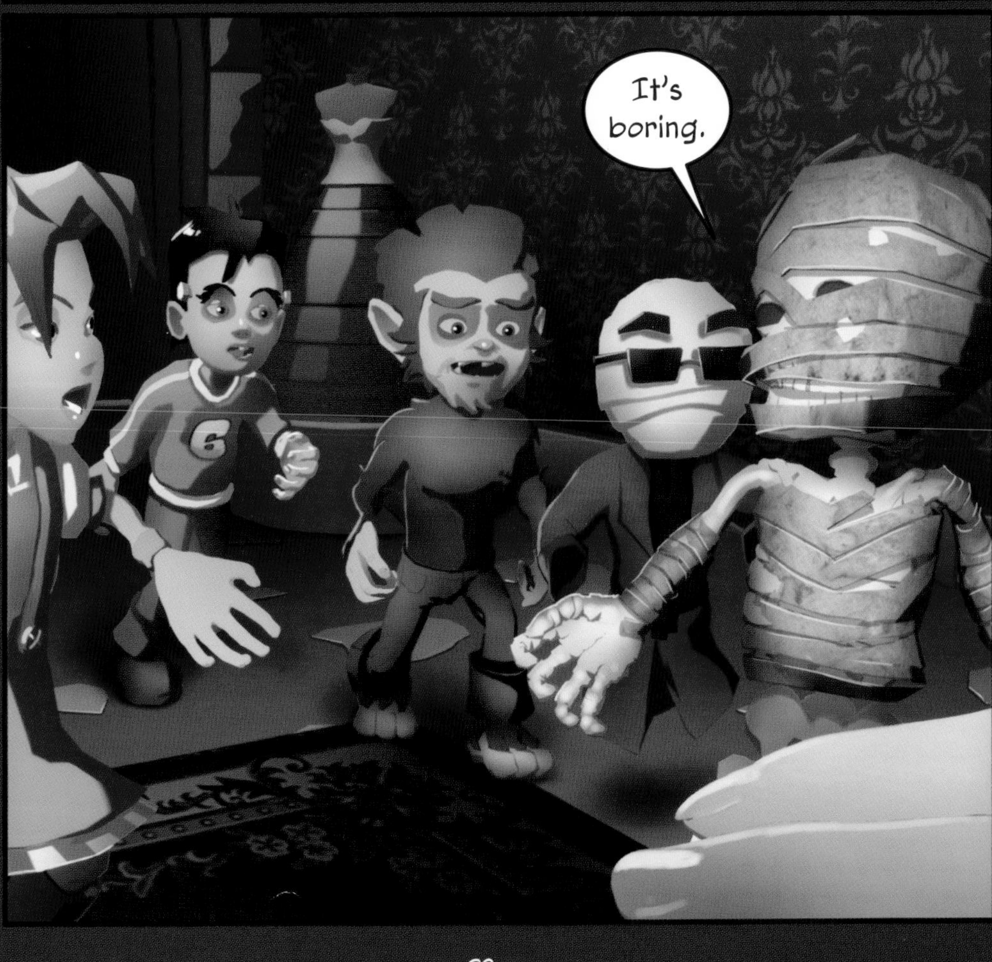
It's boring.

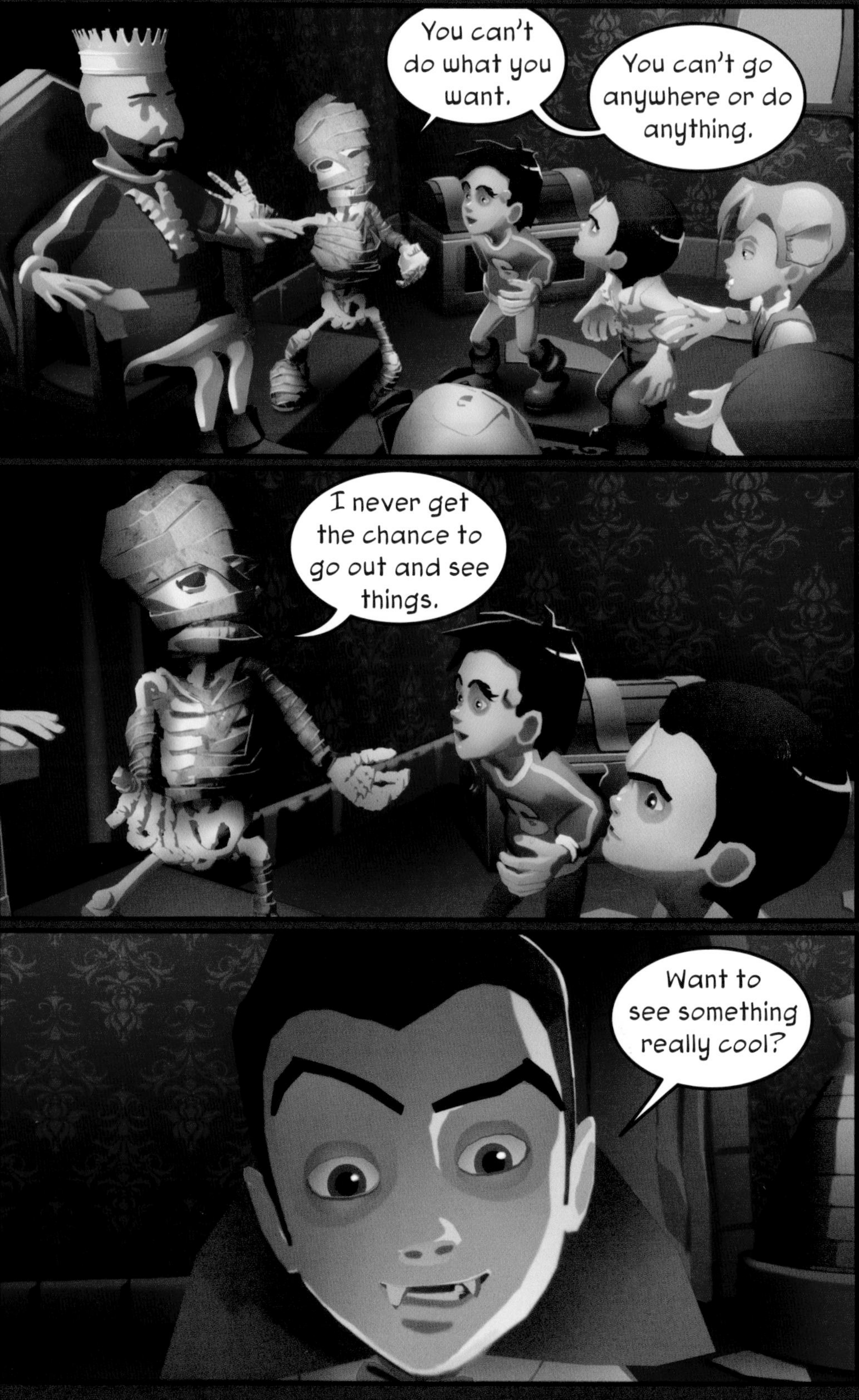
You can't do what you want.
You can't go anywhere or do anything.
I never get the chance to go out and see things.
Want to see something really cool?

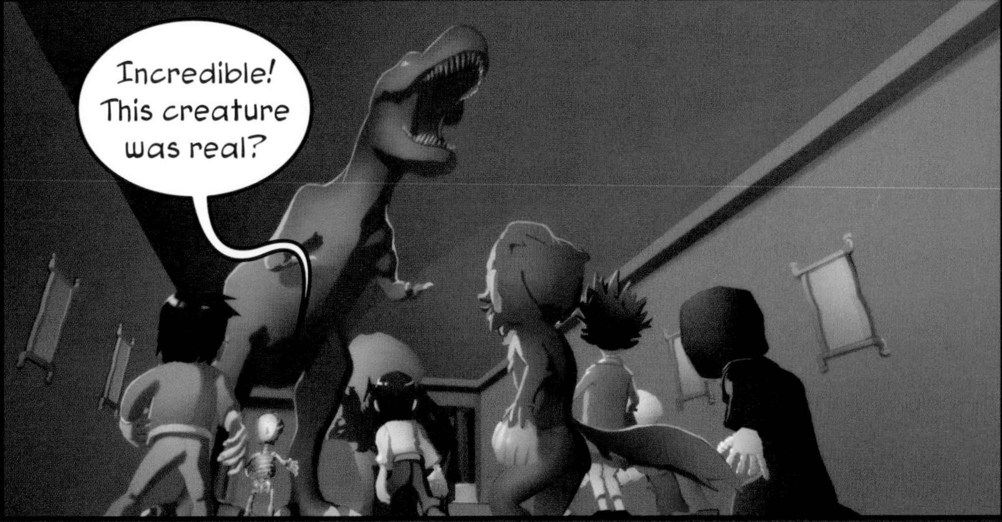
Incredible! This creature was real?

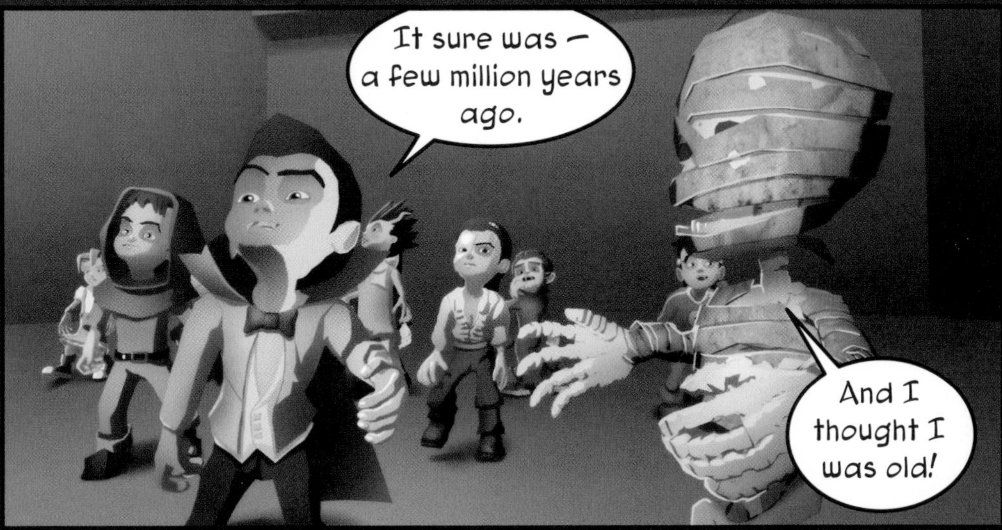
It sure was — a few million years ago.
And I thought I was old!

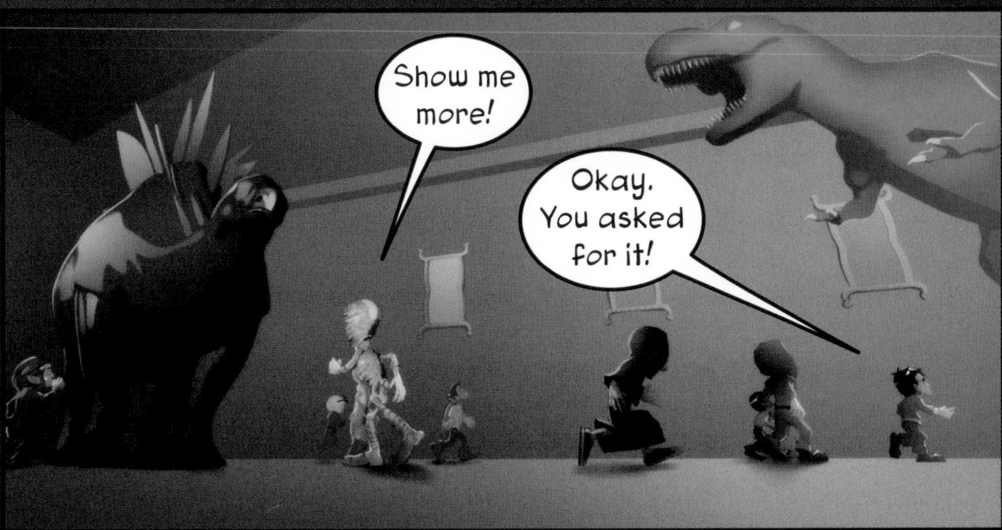
Show me more!
Okay. You asked for it!

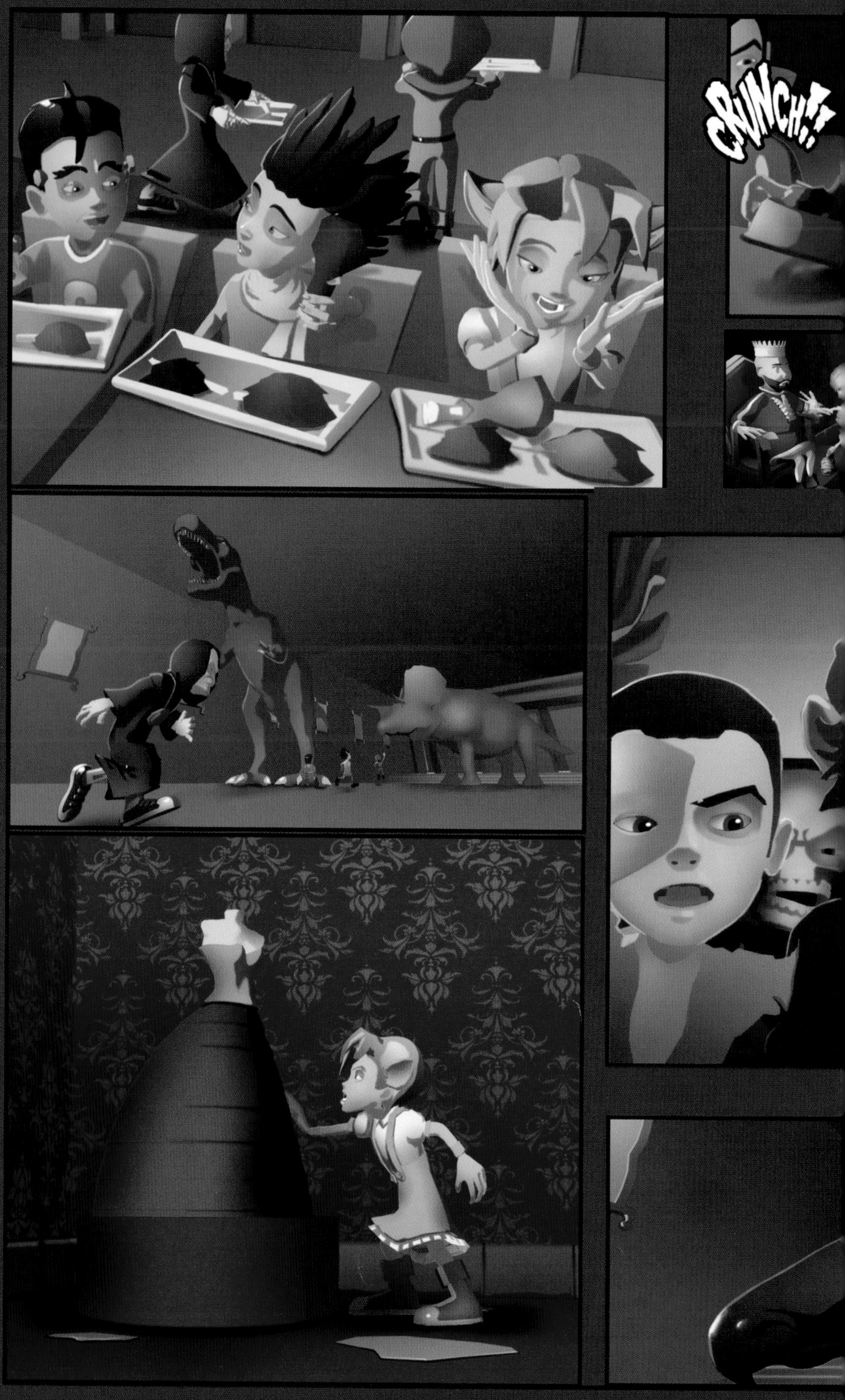
CRUNCH!!!

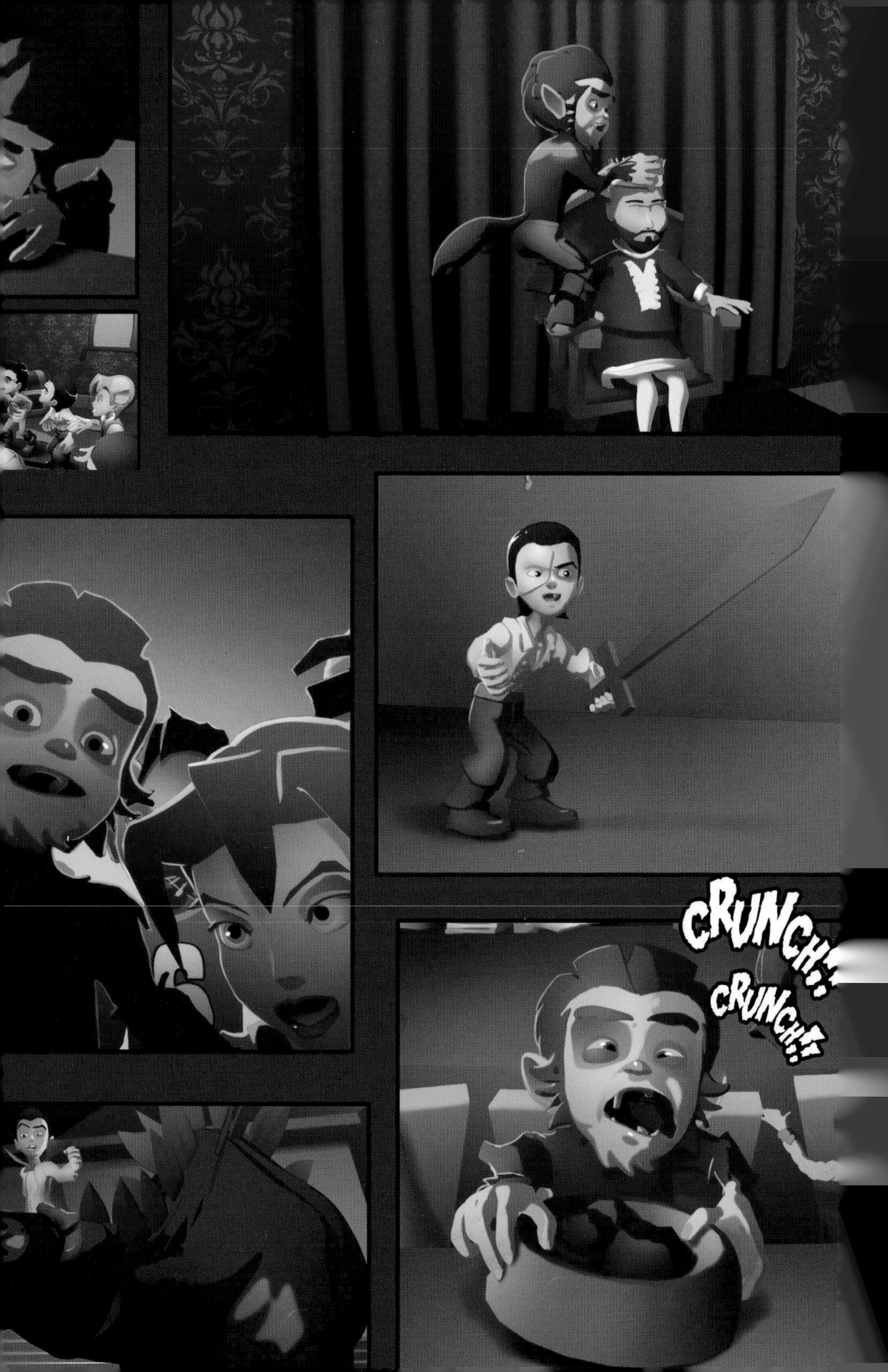
CRUNCH!!
CRUNCH!!

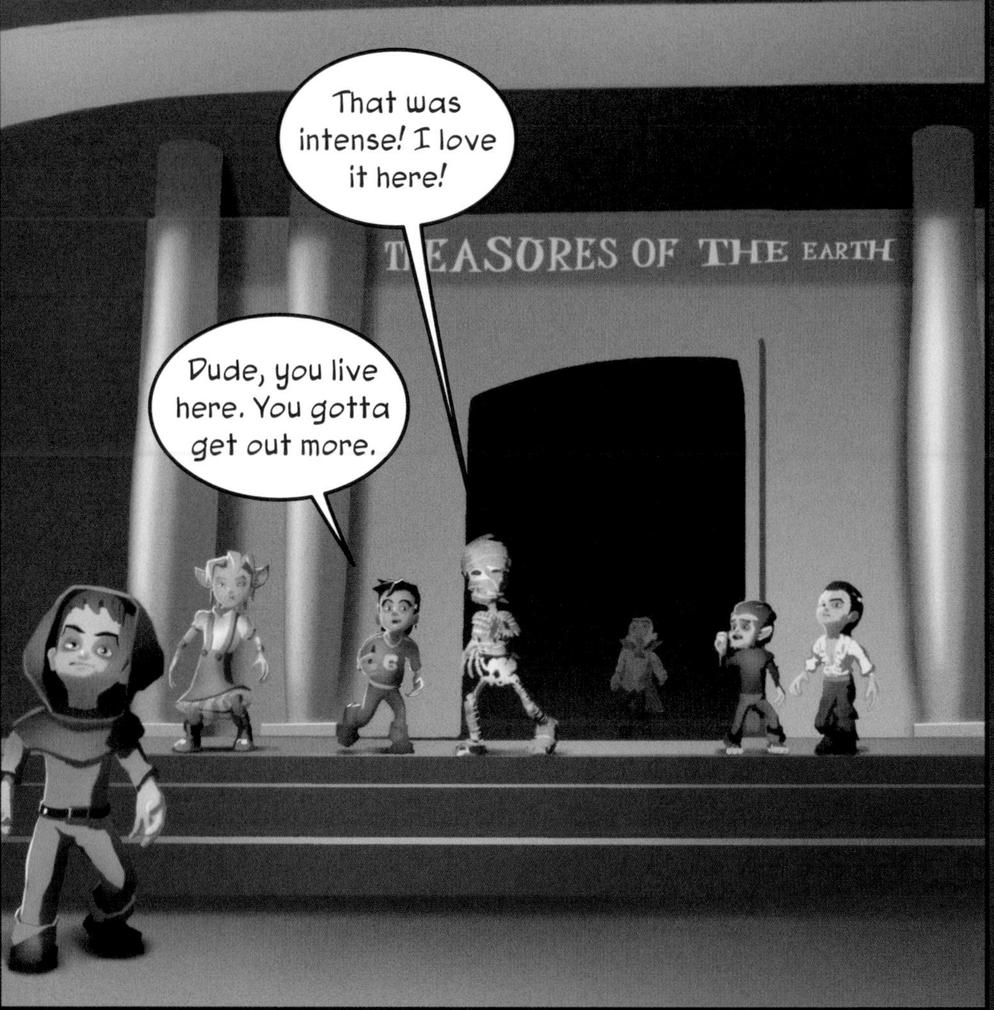
That was intense! I love it here!
Dude, you live here. You gotta get out more.

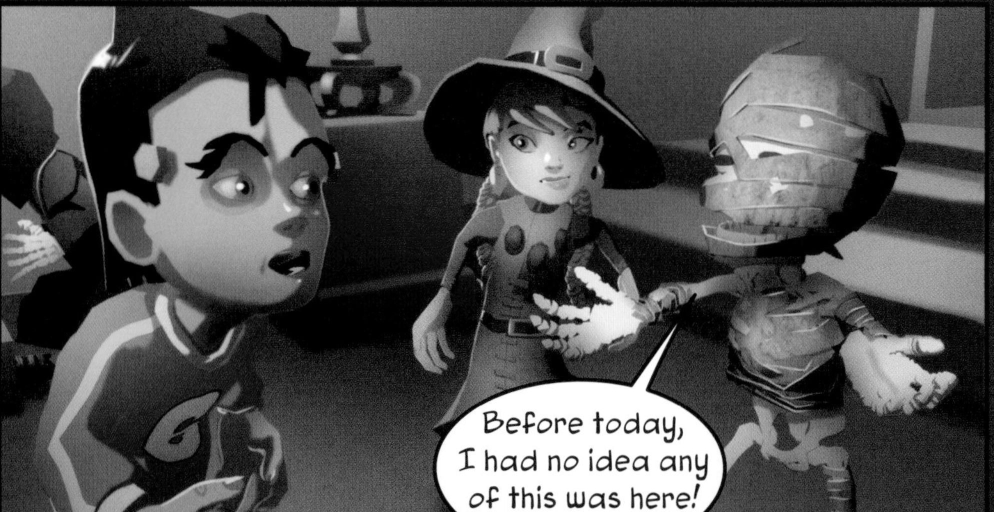
Before today, I had no idea any of this was here!

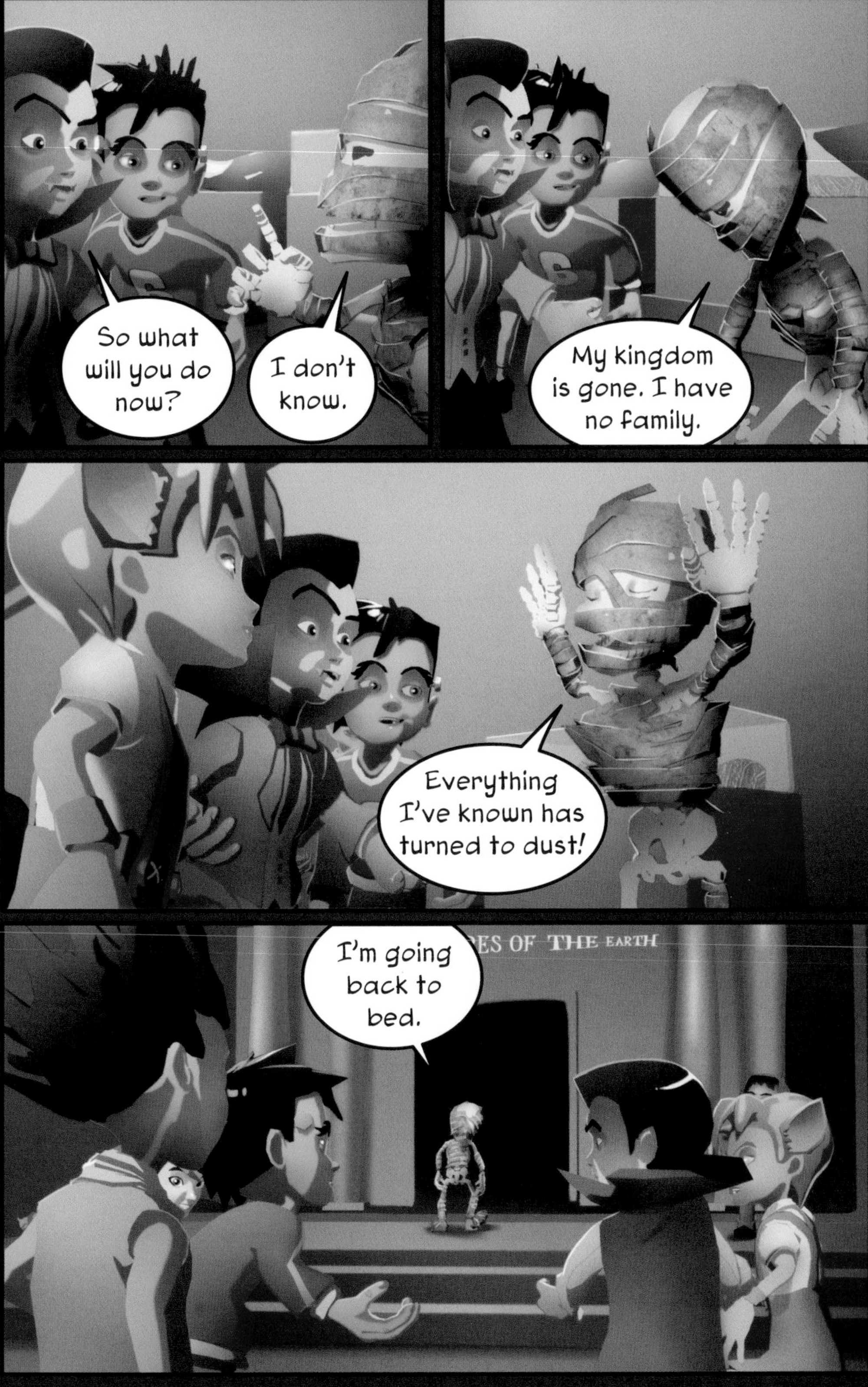
So what will you do now?
I don't know.
My kingdom is gone. I have no family.
Everything I've known has turned to dust!
...ES OF THE EARTH
I'm going back to bed.

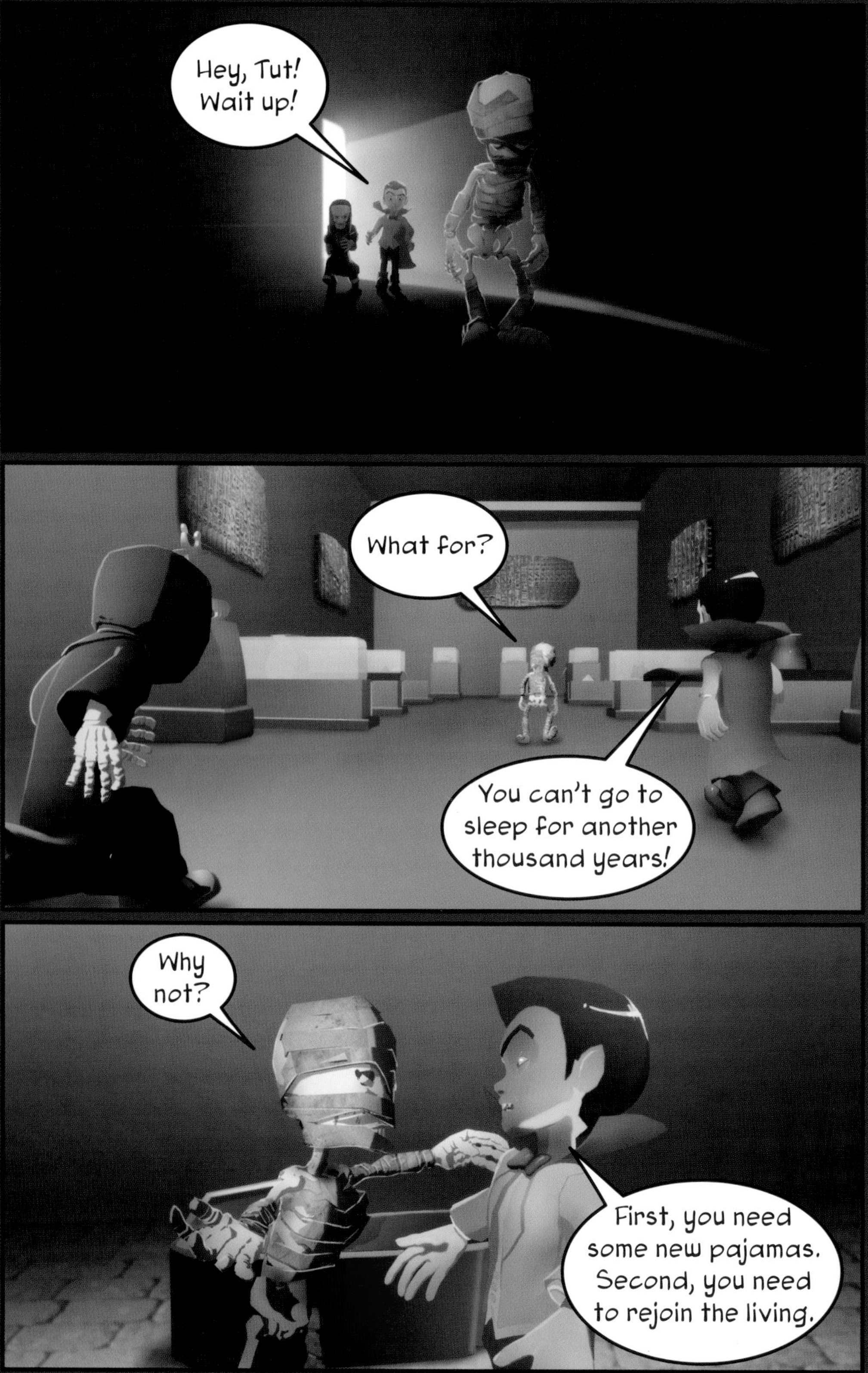
Hey, Tut! Wait up!
What for?
You can't go to sleep for another thousand years!
Why not?
First, you need some new pajamas. Second, you need to rejoin the living.

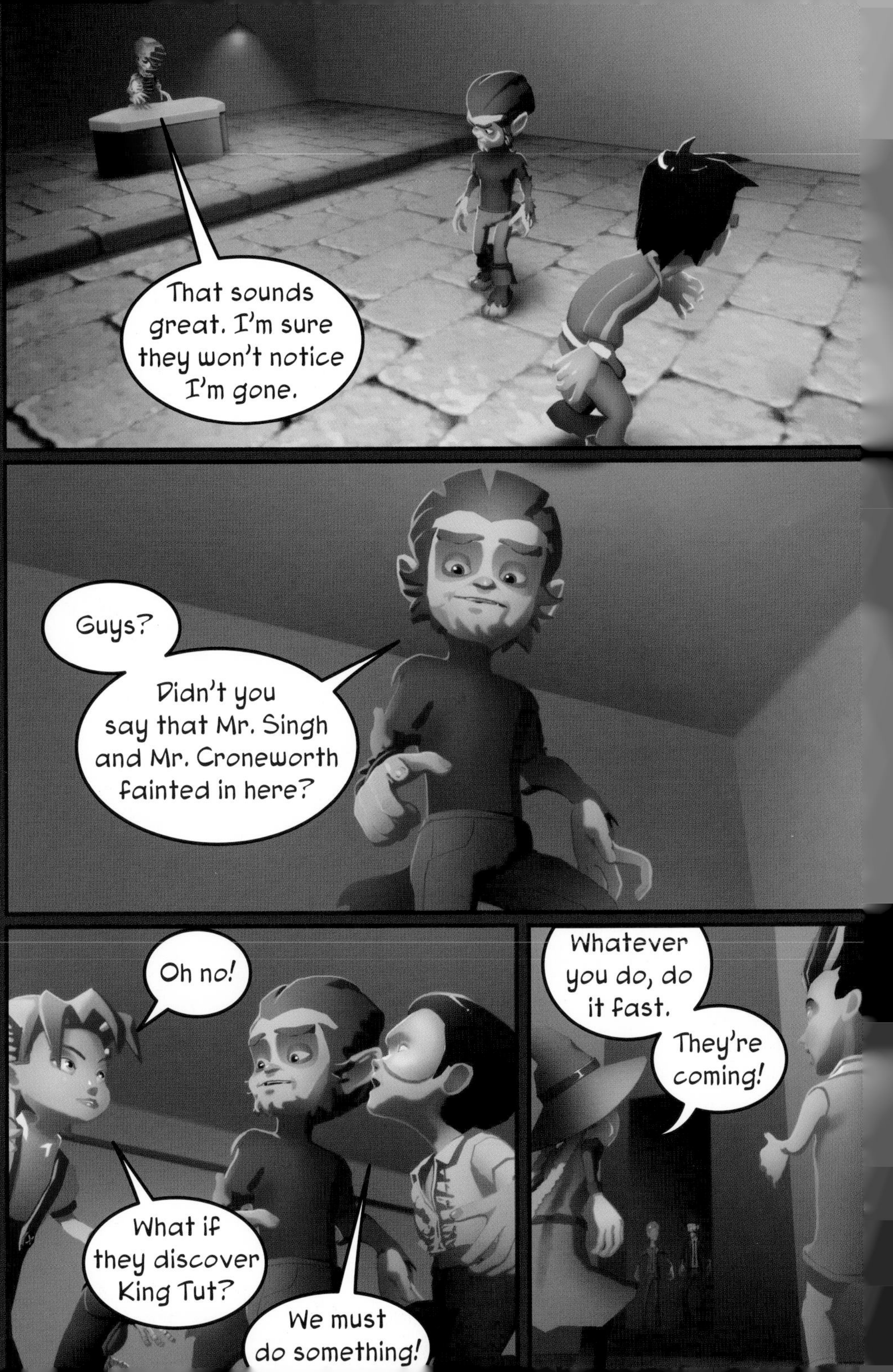
That sounds great. I'm sure they won't notice I'm gone.
Guys?
Didn't you say that Mr. Singh and Mr. Croneworth fainted in here?
Oh no!
What if they discover King Tut?
We must do something!
Whatever you do, do it fast.
They're coming!

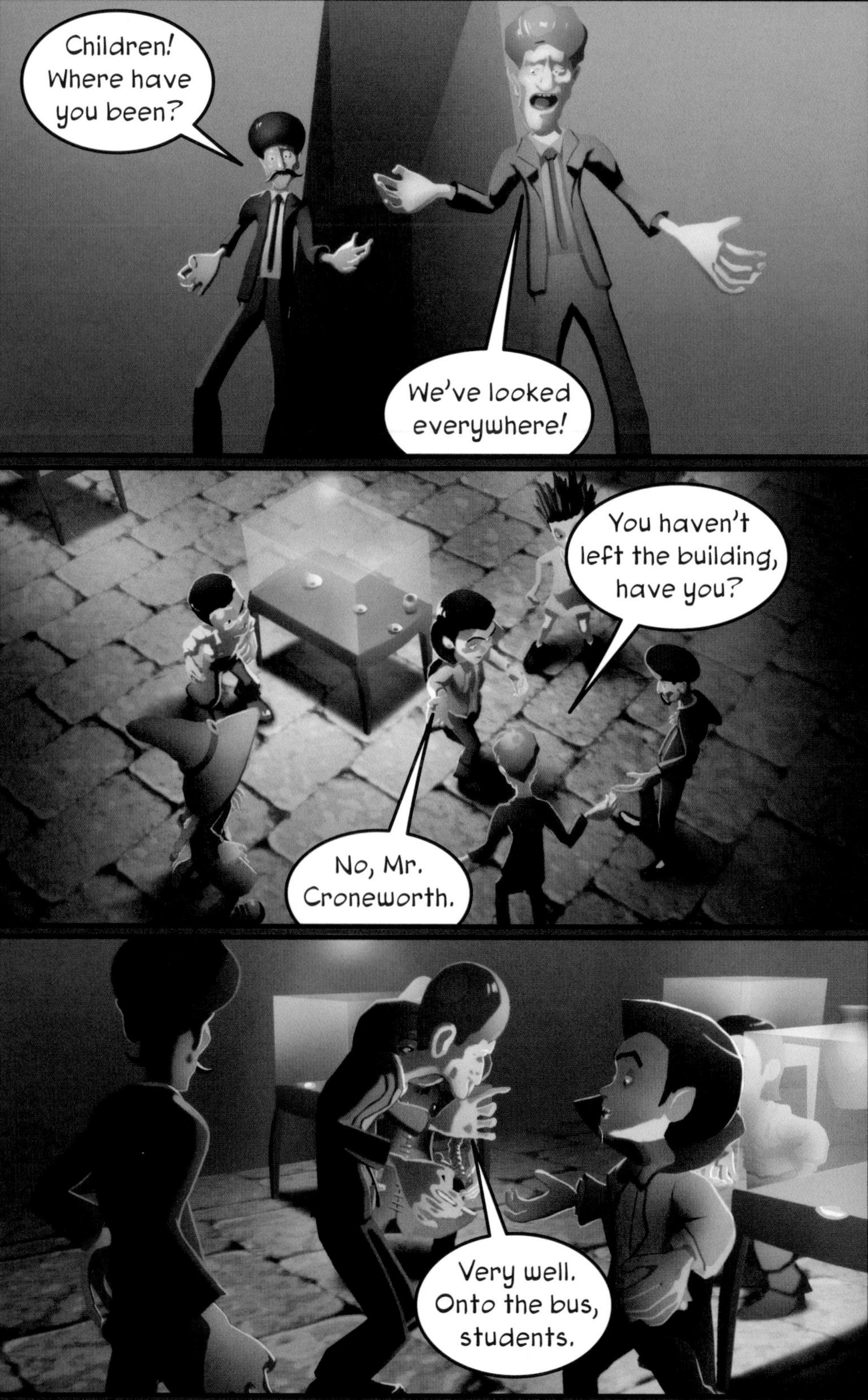
Children! Where have you been?
We've looked everywhere!
You haven't left the building, have you?
No, Mr. Croneworth.
Very well. Onto the bus, students.

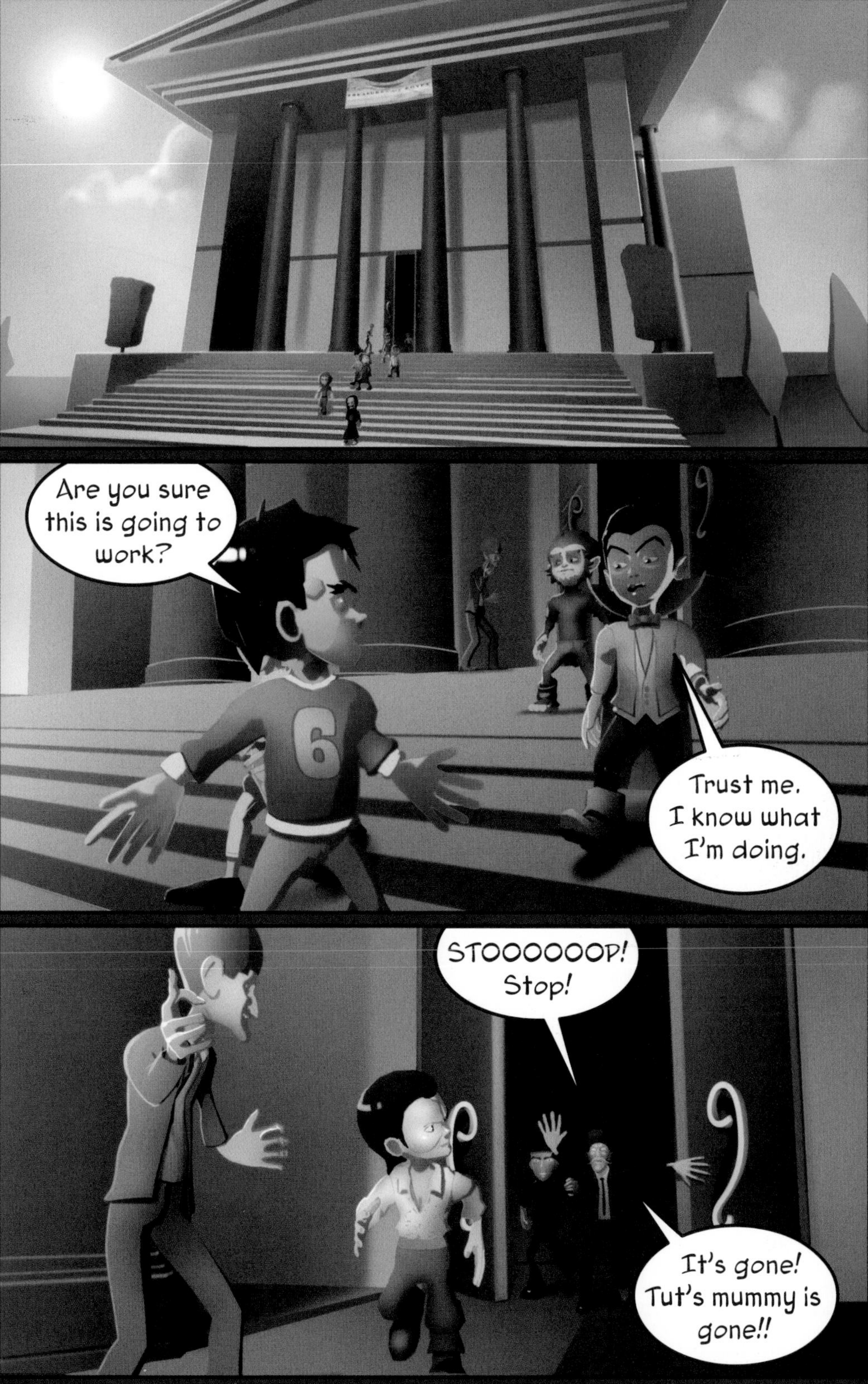

Are you sure this is going to work?
Trust me. I know what I'm doing.
STOOOOOOP! Stop!
It's gone! Tut's mummy is gone!!

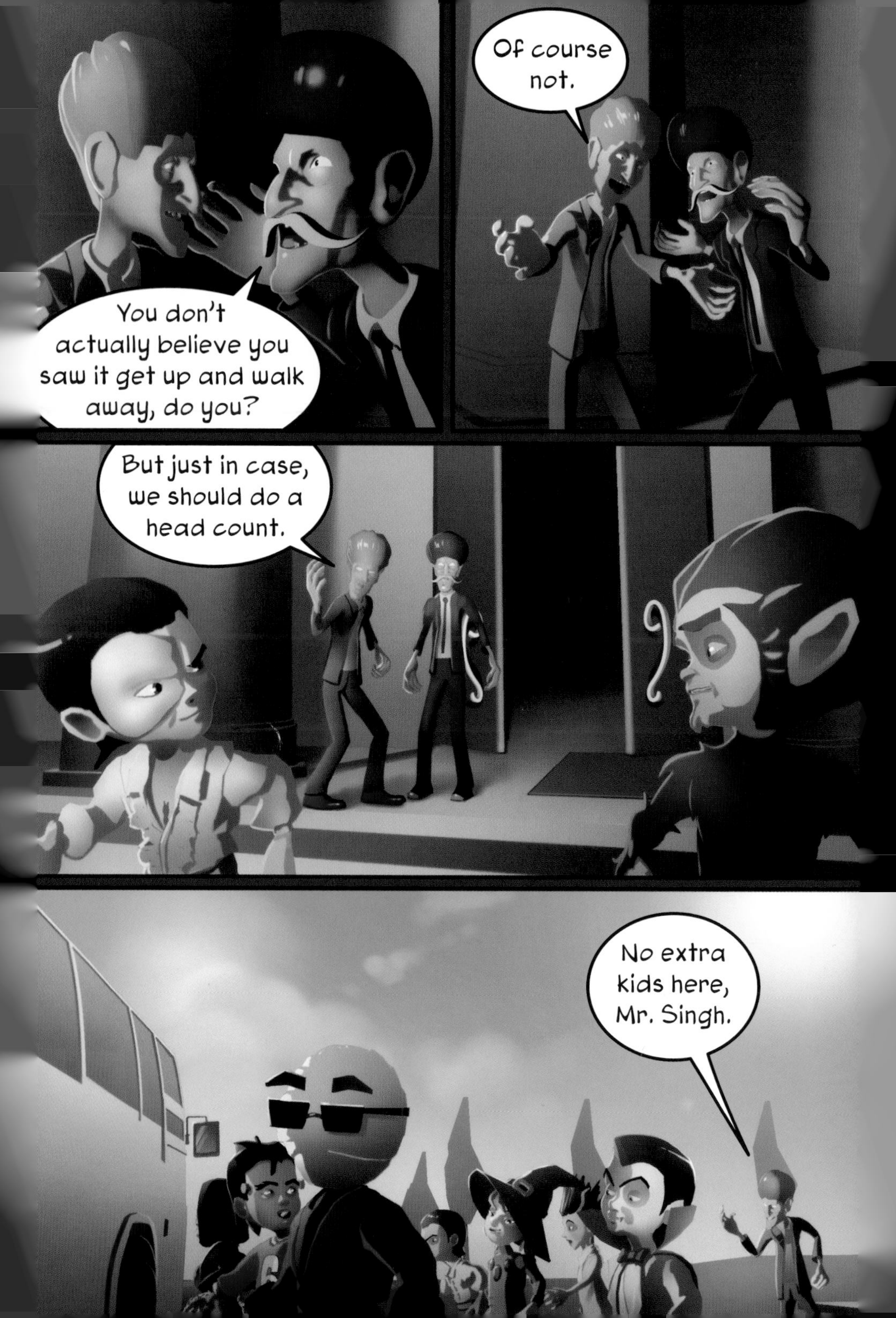
You don't actually believe you saw it get up and walk away, do you?
Of course not.
But just in case, we should do a head count.
No extra kids here, Mr. Singh.

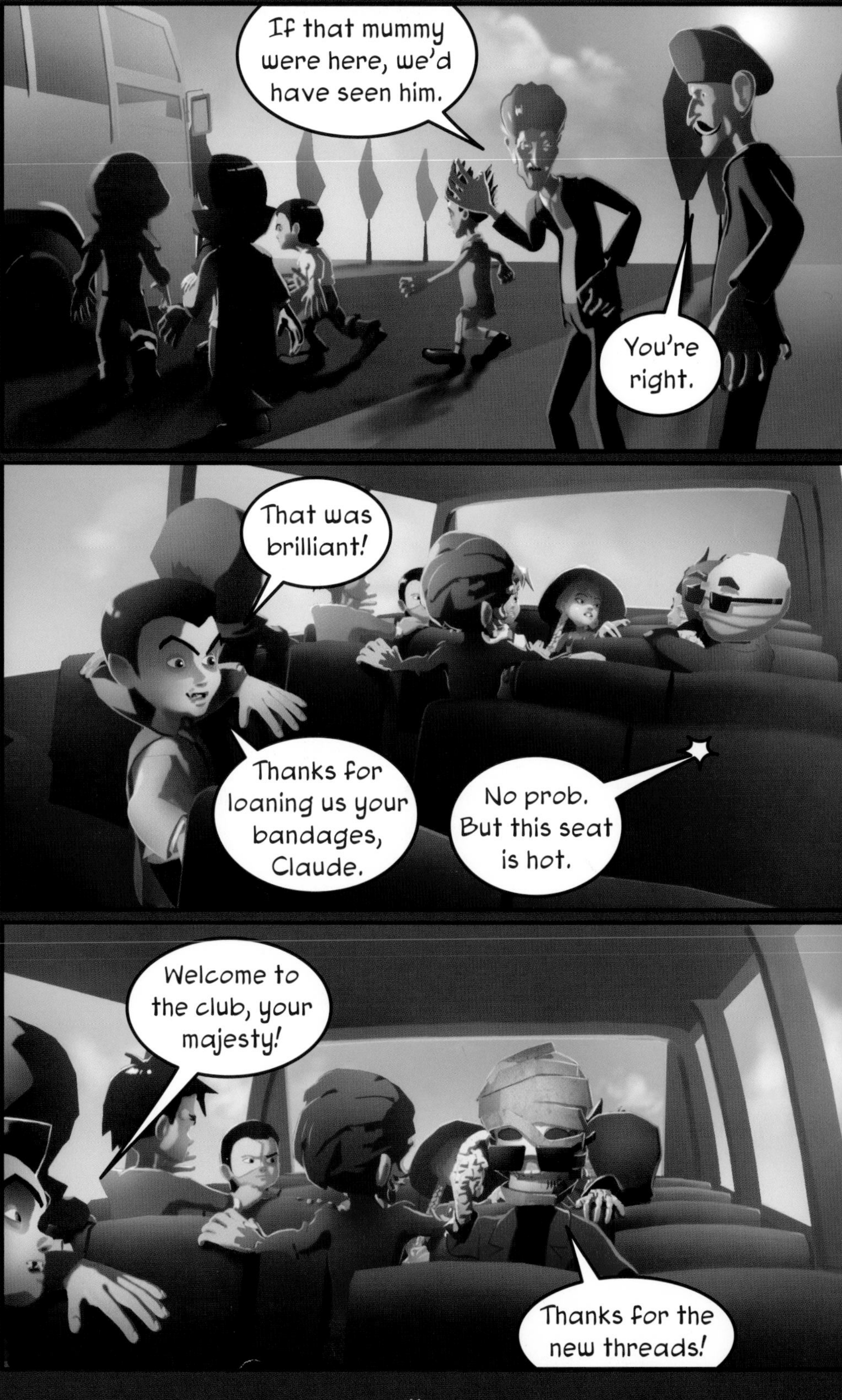
If that mummy were here, we'd have seen him.
You're right.
That was brilliant!
Thanks for loaning us your bandages, Claude.
No prob. But this seat is hot.
Welcome to the club, your majesty!
Thanks for the new threads!

WHO IS
KING TUT?

King Tut's full name is King Tutankhamun. He became king when he was just 8 or 9 years old.

King Tut married his half sister when he was just 9 years old!

Unlike pharaohs before him, King Tut did not do much for Egypt. However, the discovery of his tomb and all of his treasures has made him the most recognized and famous pharaoh of all time.

King Tut was only 18 or 19 years old when he died. It is not known what caused his death, but many scientists believe he was murdered.

In 1922, Howard Carter discovered King Tut's tomb. More than 3,000 artifacts were found inside.

GLOSSARY

ancient (AYN-shunt)—belonging to a time long ago

coffin (KAWF-in)—a container that a person is buried in

curator (KYOO-ray-tur)—the person in charge of a museum

exhibit (eg-ZIB-it)—to show something to the public

fainted (FAYNT-id)—lost consciousness for a short time

intense (in-TENSS)—very strong

introduce (in-truh-DOOSS)—to tell the name of one person to another person

kingdom (KING-duhm)—a country that has a king or queen as its ruler

majesty (MAJ-uh-stee)—the formal title for a king or a queen

monuments (MON-yuh-muhnts)—statues, buildings, or other things that are meant to remind people of an event or a person

pharaoh (FAIR-oh)—the title of kings of ancient Egypt

supervision (soo-pur-VIZH-uhn)—watch

DISCUSSION QUESTIONS

1. The Mighty Mighty Monsters took a field trip to the museum. Where would you like to go on a field trip? Why?

2. The monsters are all part of a special group. If you could be part of any group, what would it be?

3. The monsters helped King Tut escape from the museum. Do you think that was a good idea? Why or why not?

WRITING PROMPTS

1. Which monster do you like best? Write a few sentences explaining why.

2. The monsters helped King Tut and made a new friend. Write about a time when you helped a friend.

3. What happens after the monsters bring King Tut home? Write a few sentences about his life in the real world.

ABOUT
SEAN O'REILLY
AND ARCANA STUDIO

As a lifelong comics fan, Sean O'Reilly dreamed of becoming a comic book creator. In 2004, he realized that dream by creating Arcana Studio. In one short year, O'Reilly took his studio from a one-person operation in his basement to an award-winning comic book publisher with more than 150 graphic novels produced for Harper Collins, Simon & Schuster, Random House, Scholastic, and others.

Within a year, the company won many awards including the Shuster Award for Outstanding Publisher and the Moonbeam Award for top children's graphic novel. O'Reilly also won the Top 40 Under 40 award from the city of Vancouver and authored The Clockwork Girl for Top Graphic Novel at Book Expo America in 2009. Currently, O'Reilly is one of the most prolific independent comic book writers in Canada. While showing no signs of slowing down in comics, he now writes screenplays and adapts his creations for the big screen.

Mighty Mighty MONSTERS ADVENTURES

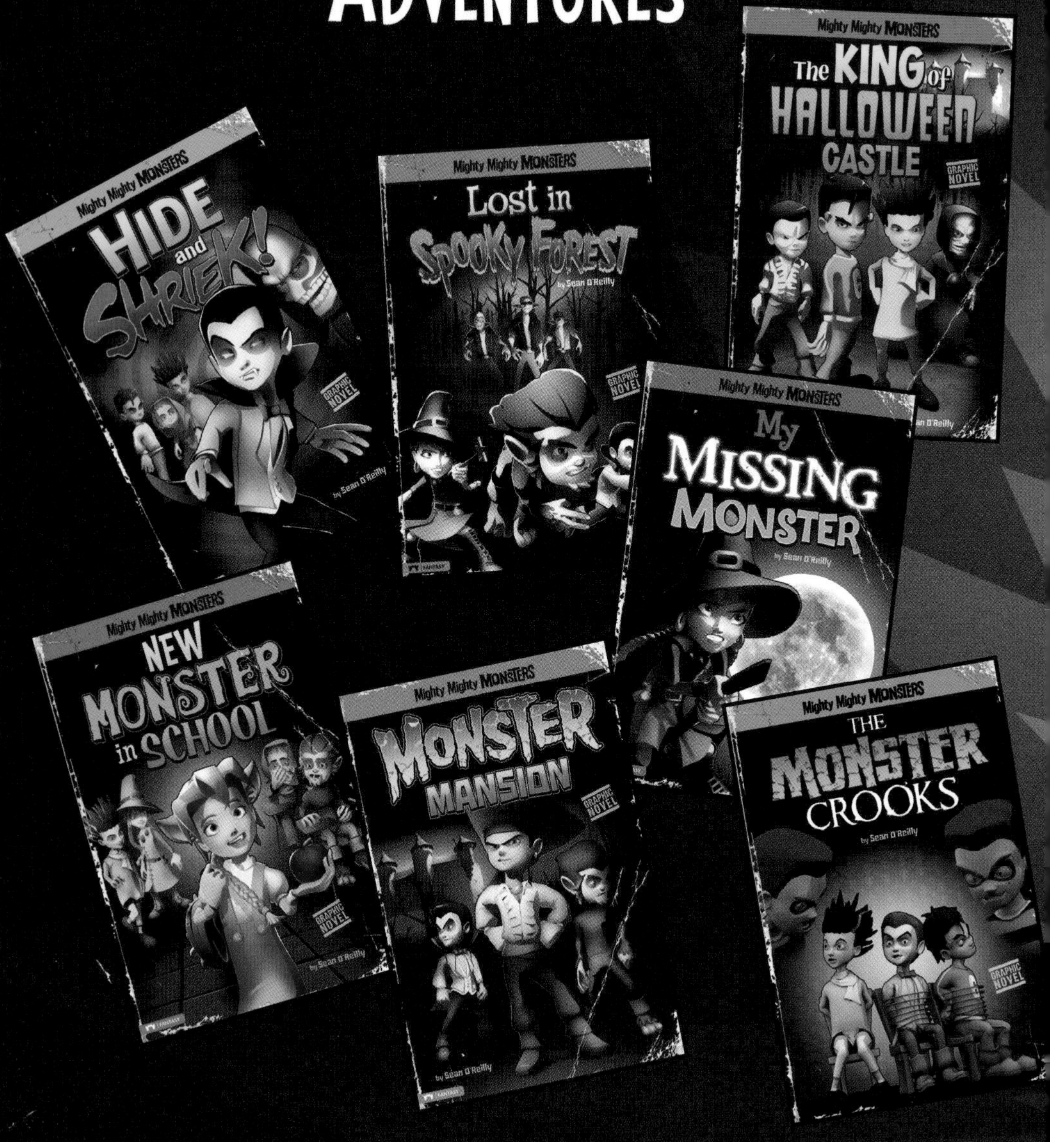

Mighty Mighty MONSTERS
HIDE and SHRIEK!
GRAPHIC NOVEL
by Sean O'Reilly
Mighty Mighty MONSTERS
Lost in Spooky Forest
by Sean O'Reilly
GRAPHIC NOVEL
Mighty Mighty MONSTERS
The KING of HALLOWEEN CASTLE
GRAPHIC NOVEL
Mighty Mighty MONSTERS
My MISSING MONSTER
by Sean O'Reilly
Mighty Mighty MONSTERS
NEW MONSTER in SCHOOL
GRAPHIC NOVEL
by Sean O'Reilly
Mighty Mighty MONSTERS
MONSTER MANSION
GRAPHIC NOVEL
by Sean O'Reilly
Mighty Mighty MONSTERS
THE MONSTER CROOKS
by Sean O'Reilly
GRAPHIC NOVEL

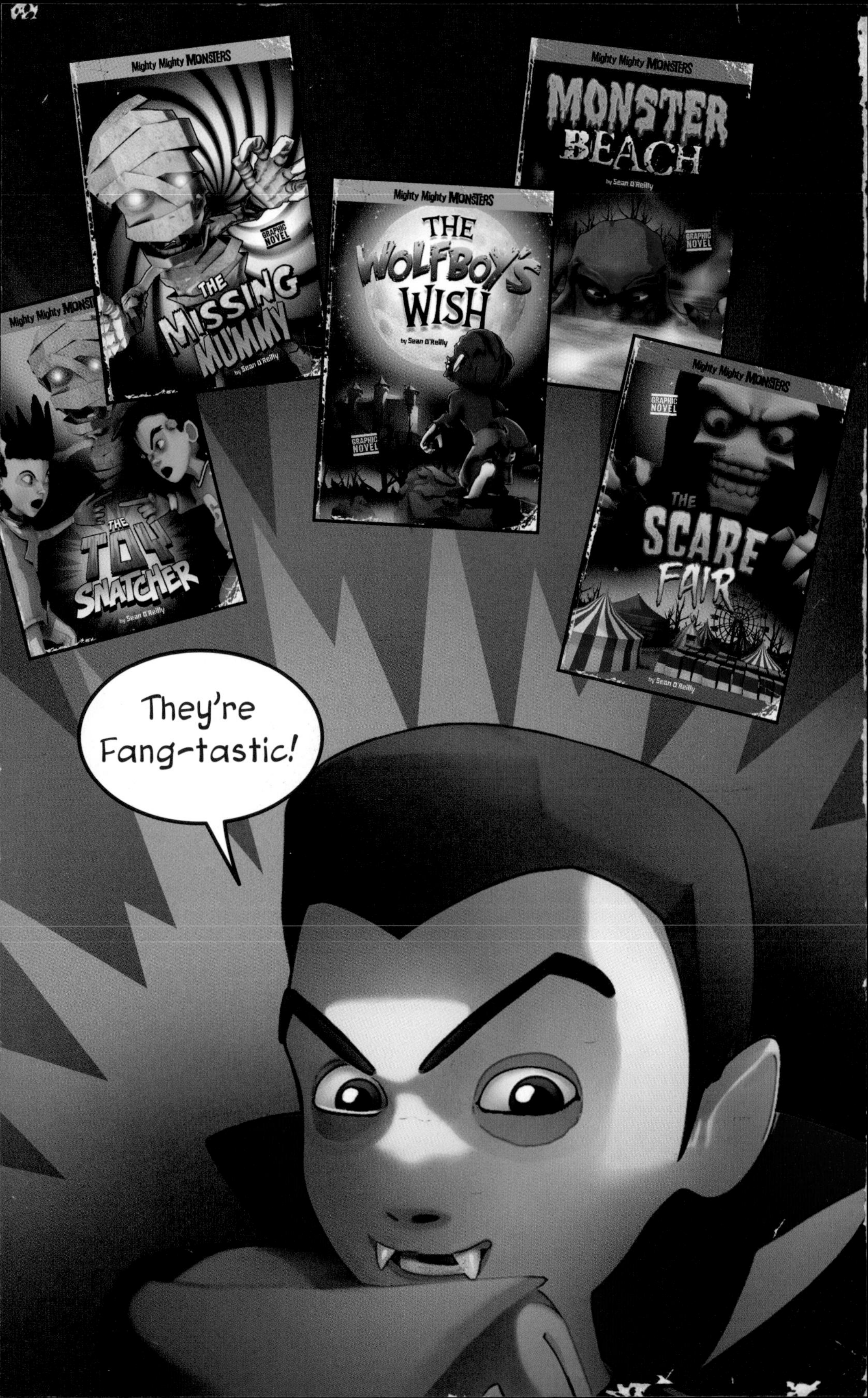
Mighty Mighty MONSTERS
THE MISSING MUMMY
by Sean O'Reilly
GRAPHIC NOVEL
Mighty Mighty MONSTERS
THE WOLFBOY'S WISH
by Sean O'Reilly
GRAPHIC NOVEL
Mighty Mighty MONSTERS
MONSTER BEACH
by Sean O'Reilly
GRAPHIC NOVEL
Mighty Mighty MONSTERS
THE TOY SNATCHER
by Sean O'Reilly
Mighty Mighty MONSTERS
GRAPHIC NOVEL
THE SCARE FAIR
by Sean O'Reilly
They're Fang-tastic!